DISCLAIMER

This contemporary romantic suspense contains adult themes such as power exchange and sexual scenes. Please do not read if these offend you.

DEDICATION

I would like to thank my cover designer, Joe Dugdale, who worked with me to get the cover I wanted and to Sylv, my PA who keeps me sane, I view her as my personal publisher but I have complete control.

You can contact them yourself at Sylv.net (www. sylv.net)

PROTECTOR

DOMS OF MOUNTAIN BEND

BOOK 1

BJ Wane

Editors:
Kate Richards & Nanette Sipes

Cover Design & Formatting:
Joe Dugdale (sylv.net)

CONTENTS

PROLOGUE

"This is going to put a kink in our plans." Shawn eased the bedroom door closed and turned to his two friends. "Now what?" he whispered, wincing as he raised his right hand to brush his hair out of his eyes, forgetting about his sprained wrist for a minute.

"I don't see how this changes anything."

Clayton paced the worn carpet in the bedroom the three of them had shared since arriving at the Atkins' foster home, his black eye almost swollen shut. It wasn't the first time Clayton's penchant for arguing had ignited Doyle Atkins' short fuse. Then again, they'd learned the first week it didn't take much to set off their foster parent. Doyle had already revealed his angry, abusive nature to Shawn with a fist to his gut by the time Clayton and Dakota were relocated to the Atkins house a month after him. At fifteen, all three of them were deemed too incorrigible and too old for adoption, and were expected to hang out here for another two years before the state would consider turning them loose on society.

They all agreed on one thing – fuck that, they were out of here now.

"What about her?" Shawn nodded toward the door and the low murmur of voices they could still hear coming from the living room.

Dakota drilled him with a black-eyed glare. "What do you suggest, McDuff, that we drag a kid around the streets with us when we don't even know where we're going yet?"

Shawn dropped onto his bed with a muttered, frustrated curse. "Of course not, you imbecile."

"Mrs. Atkins will return in a few days. She'll be fine until then."

Shawn noticed Clayton's assertion didn't match the concern in his blue eyes, not that it mattered. They were both determined to stick with the plan to sneak out of here tonight. Their meager belongings were stuffed in their backpacks, and each of them had agreed to their designated role. Dakota, with his height advantage and larger frame, could hold his own against Doyle better than either Shawn or Clayton, so he would stand guard after the old man succumbed to his nightly drunken stupor. Clayton would head to the kitchen to fill plastic bags with food, and he would grab Doyle's cash stash from his office, everyone meeting behind the house within five minutes.

"You don't know that," Shawn shot back. The last thing they'd expected this evening was the arrival of a new foster kid from social services. He'd only gotten a glimpse of the blonde-haired little girl who couldn't be more than seven or eight, but his stomach had clenched at the gleam in Doyle's eyes as Shawn had walked by the ajar door to the living room. "I say we wait a few days, just until Mrs. Atkins returns."

Dakota snorted with derision, his look scathing as he retorted, "Why? She never intervened between her husband and us."

"She wanted girls, not teenage boys. I say..."

Clayton held up a hand. "We vote on it, like always.

I say we keep to our original plan and go tonight. Dakota?"

"I'm with you. Tonight."

Shawn blew out a frustrated breath then sighed, having no choice but to go along. "Fine," he agreed, wishing there was another option. But in the three years since his father had been killed in the line of duty, he'd learned wishing never amounted to a hill of beans.

Five hours later, the three of them ventured out of their room into the now darkened house. They hadn't expected Atkins to check on them, not even to see if they'd eaten anything for dinner or to introduce them to the new kid. The little girl's soft voice as she'd talked to herself filtered through the thin walls from her room for a time following the social worker's departure, but all had been silent for the last thirty minutes.

"Meet you in five out back," Dakota whispered before pivoting and disappearing around the corner of the hall.

"It's spooky, how fucking quiet he is when he moves." Clayton shook his head. "Quit pouting, McDuff. This is a new start for us if we can get out of here undetected."

"I'm not pouting. Go. Don't forget my sunflower seeds."

"As if. Good luck, man."

Clayton headed in the same direction as Dakota while Shawn crept down the hall toward the last room on the right. A muffled sound from the little girl's room made him pause then he kept going when he heard nothing else. As he slipped into Atkins' office and pried open the locked desk drawer, he hoped his dad wasn't watching. Patrick McDuff had taught Shawn to respect the law and to stand for the victims of those who broke it. As a single dad, Patrick had also raised him to do what was necessary to make the best of a bad situation and taught him to fend for himself at a young age. He could take care of himself once they were away from this place and the authorities.

Shawn grabbed the locked metal box and tucked it under his arm. It was only sheer luck he'd caught a glimpse of what the cash box held when he'd entered the room without knocking his second day here. That was the first time he'd earned a punishment with Atkins' fist. He dashed into the hall but slowed his step as he neared the little girl's room, her soft cry drawing an icy shiver down his spine, her voice a tiny whimper that stirred his anger.

"No, go away, *please stop!*"

Without thinking, he barged into the room, took in the scene of Atkins leaning over her on the bed, his hand fumbling with her nightgown as he mumbled drunken curses. For the first time, Shawn understood the term "seeing red" and brought the box down on the bastard's head. Grabbing Doyle by the back of his shirt, he shoved him to the floor, taking a moment to ensure he was out cold before turning to the cowering child.

With his heart pounding and no time to spare, he gave her two choices. "I can take you somewhere safe, or you can stay here. What do you want to do? We have to hurry."

She gulped, her green eyes wide with shock and

an indefinable emotion he couldn't name. Then she surprised the hell out of him when she launched herself at him and clung to his neck with her frail little arms.

"I want to...to go...with you. *Please.*"

Shawn shuddered, praying he was doing the right thing as he snatched the blanket off the bed and draped it around her shivering body. "Let's go."

He ran through the house and out the rear kitchen door, no longer worried about waking Atkins but about his friends' reaction. The moment they saw him coming out the door, Dakota cursed a blue streak.

"What the hell are you thinking?" Clayton asked, his eyes showing the briefest compassion as he looked at the little girl huddling against Shawn.

"He was in her room." Apparently they both read his expression correctly because they backed off, Dakota's eyes going stone cold as they rested on the girl's blonde head, all that was visible of her under the blanket.

"What are you going to do with her now?"

Shawn swallowed, never liking it when a hint of Dakota's rough upbringing on the Indian reservation came through in that soft, controlled voice. The guy could be downright scary.

"I'll take her to Father Joe's and meet up with you at the diner."

"No," Clayton said. "We're a team; we stay together. Dakota?"

"Like you said, we're a team. Come on, let's move."

Shawn handed the metal box to Dakota and set off on foot for the rectory at St. Luke's Church, grateful for their support. He'd talked a lot about Father Joe in the months since the three of them had bonded. The priest and his father were best friends, going back to their high school days, and Father Joe had been the closest person to family Shawn could claim. Their relationship wasn't enough to keep him out of the foster care system, but at least he had support whenever he needed someone he could rely on.

The church was a good two miles from the Atkins' neighborhood, and hiking that distance in the Arizona summer night heat while staying off high-traffic roads was exhausting. They didn't converse much, saving their energy, each of them worried about the little girl's silence. Her small body still quivered against Shawn's chest, her ragged breathing on his neck compelling him to maintain his tight hold. By the time they reached the rear door of the rectory, sweaty and tired, she had fallen asleep.

Clayton rapped on the door and stepped to the side, letting Shawn take the lead when Father Joe answered.

"Shawn! What's going on? Are you all right?" Opening the door wider, the priest waved them in.

"Father, this is Clayton and Dakota, the friends I've told you about. I don't know her name, but we can't take her with us." Shawn let his urgency come through in his voice as he didn't know how long they had until Atkins roused and alerted the cops.

Father Joe nudged up his wire-frame glasses and looked them over with a critical eye, his mouth tightening as he spotted Clayton's bruised face and Shawn's wrapped wrist. "I'll contact social services in the morning and insist they move you."

Dakota went rigid. "No."

Shawn shifted the little girl as she roused, lifting her head to peer at him out of frightened round eyes. "Don't talk so mean," he snapped at Dakota before telling her, "It's okay. He's nice, but he doesn't want anyone to know that. Father Joe is going to take care of you, isn't that right, Father? It would be a shame if she was sent back to that house where she's not safe."

No one knew him better than the priest, and Shawn released a relieved breath when Father Joe read between the lines correctly and nodded. He'd tried to talk Shawn into relocating to one of his out-of-state contacts following his father's death, but he'd refused. Phoenix had been home his whole life, and he'd already lost so much that, at the time, he couldn't stomach another upheaval.

Moving so the girl could see him, Father Joe used his gentlest tone to talk to her. "I know a very nice family who would love to have you. Would you like to meet them?"

Instead of answering, she looked at Shawn. "Will you be there?"

"No, I have to go somewhere else, but I promise you'll be safe. Didn't I save you from the bad man?" She gave him a reluctant nod and loosened her clinging arms from around his neck. "Good girl." He smiled, setting her on her feet. Laying a hand on her head, he said, "You keep being good, and everything will be fine. Right, Father?"

"Right, as long as the three of you agree to my terms."

"Shit," Dakota mumbled, turning to lean against

the wall with his arms folded, his glare solely for Shawn.

Shawn recognized the determined glint in Father Joe's eyes, wondering how he could have not considered this possibility. "C'mon, man, you can't mean to blackmail us."

"Oh, but I can," Father Joe returned, Shawn recognizing his implacable tone.

Wearing worn jeans and an Arizona Cardinals tee shirt, he didn't look anything like a priest in his mid-forties, but Shawn knew that look, and he meant what he said. If he wanted his help, Shawn would have to agree to his terms.

"You trusted me enough to come here tonight. All I'm asking is you trust me enough to do right by all of you, not just the little one. Agreed?" His gaze circled to include the three of them.

"What's to keep us from bolting once we agree?" Clayton asked with a rare touch of belligerence. Most often, he was the easy-going one between them.

"Smarts enough to know when you've been handed a second chance, and the grit to make the most of it," Father Joe challenged in reply.

"Well, hell."

Clayton flipped Dakota a wry grin then looked at Shawn. "If he's in, I'm in."

Shawn ran his hand down the girl's silky hair, his heart somersaulting over the adoring look she turned up to him. "Okay, Father. If you see she stays safe, we agree. Where are we going?"

"Idaho."

CHAPTER ONE

Twenty years later

"Are you sure, Randy?"

Shawn McDuff took the pen his friend handed over, his gaze skimming the now quiet, empty cavernous room of the private club, Spurs. He recalled the fond memory of a scene with a redheaded submissive when his eyes landed on the St. Andrew's Cross. He, Clayton, and Dakota had been members since Randy first opened the club over seven years ago. Located just outside of Boise, it sat nestled in a tree-shrouded copse in between Boise and Mountain Bend, the small town they now called home.

"I'm sure. I've known you guys long enough to have complete confidence you'll ensure Spurs keeps the good reputation I've worked to build," Randy replied, his look around the table taking in Shawn, Clayton, and Dakota.

Scrawling his name on the contract to buy the club, Shawn was confident of the asset they were purchasing, but the disillusionment in Randy's eyes was still hard to see. He couldn't imagine the heartache of betrayal his friend must feel over his wife's infidelity and desertion.

"It helps Shawn is a deputy sheriff." Clayton balanced his chair on the back two legs with ease, his arms crossed, blue eyes lit with humor. "He'll threaten anyone who gets out of line with jail time."

Dakota snorted. "Some subs will act up so he'll do just that."

"Kathie. That girl lives to get in trouble with the Masters." Shawn handed the pen to Dakota, thinking of the blonde who was an attention seeker, but harmless. "What are your plans now, Randy?"

Pushing to his feet, Randy said, "I haven't been out of Idaho in years, and there are several places I've always wanted to visit. These will unlock the front and rear doors, and the smaller one goes to the storage closet in the corner." He tossed down a set of keys and picked up the cashier's check and signed copy of the sale. "You know how to reach me if you have any problems or questions, but seeing as you've been members since the doors opened, I doubt there's anything you'll need my help with. Thanks." He held out his hand, and they each stood to accept his shake.

"Keep in touch." Shawn released his grip, hoping Randy found the peace of mind he was looking for in his travels.

"Will do. I want to check out the second floor you're planning on adding. I know several people have asked for private rooms but never thought of taking advantage of the high ceiling space to add an entire floor." Picking up his Stetson, Randy settled it on his head and walked out without looking back.

"Poor bastard. Just another reason to stay unattached."

"You don't need another reason, Clay," Shawn returned, reaching for his whiskey as he resumed his seat. "Last I heard, the sun rising each morning was enough for you to stay single."

Clayton shrugged, lowering onto his chair with a thud. "Why settle for one piece of decadent chocolate when I can have the whole box?"

Dakota gave Clayton a derisive glance. "At least I have the excuse of scaring them off. Once they get what they want from me, they can't scamper away fast enough, which is fine by me." He reached for the bottle in the center of the table and topped off his glass then passed it over to Shawn.

Shawn capped it and rose to return it to the bar. Unlike his two best friends, he wouldn't mind finding one woman he could settle down with. But, ever since the three of them had inherited a portion of Buck Cooper's estate, his dates seemed more interested in learning why he continued working as a deputy sheriff, and with learning exactly how much the wealthy rancher left them. He didn't waste his time telling them their foster parent had instilled in each of them a strong work ethic, taught them the value of earning their money, and to take pride in what they accomplish.

They had money, enough he could quit his job and work the ranch putting in fewer hours. But he loved the law, got a sense of satisfaction out of enforcing it so others could live in safety. Nothing pissed him off faster than seeing an innocent person suffer from another's illegal actions.

Shawn grabbed his hat off the bar top and returned to the table, ready to call it a night. "Let's head out. The architect will be here first thing in the morning."

"I'll be in court in Boise, so take notes for me, will you?" Clayton asked, scraping back his chair. "What do you think Buck would have said about us owning a kink club?"

"As long as we stayed this side of the law, he would have said go for it, the same as he and Miss Betty told us every time one of us would wrestle with a decision."

Shawn still missed the big, gruff rancher who had taken the three of them in all those years ago. What he and Clayton and Dakota had suffered before coming to Idaho, Buck Cooper and his wife had made up for in spades. Buck taught them everything they needed to learn about ranching and farming crops in the Gem State, and Miss Betty had tempered the hard work and strict rules with unabashed warm hugs and lots of home cooking. The contrast between the rough-around-the- edges tough rancher and his soft-spoken, always smiling wife had at first amused them, prompting them to push their buttons. But it hadn't taken long for them to learn their usual tactics of lashing out against the authority figures who had taken over their lives weren't going to work this time.

Buck's sudden death from a massive heart attack two years ago had devastated them and Miss Betty. When his will was read, leaving his wife financially well-off and the entire fifty-thousand plus acre ranch to Shawn, Clayton, and Dakota, they'd vowed to continue making the generous couple proud.

"Shawn ought to worry more about what Father Joe would say," Dakota said in a scoffing tone.

"Father doesn't judge, just lectures. Still, that might be one sin I omit the next time I go to him for confession," Shawn replied as they stepped outside, humor lacing his voice.

He drew in a deep breath of cool spring air as they strode toward Dakota's Jeep, the only vehicle in the gravel parking lot. The ink-black, star-studded sky was the same as in Arizona, but that was the only common denominator between the two states where he had lived. The much colder temperatures had taken getting used to coming from such a hot, arid climate, but now he much preferred the mountains, towering pines, and endless ranges to the cacti-strewn, sandy desert. Whenever he took the time to visit Father Joe, his only connection now to Phoenix, he found he didn't miss his childhood home turf anymore.

"He came through for us when we needed him to," Clayton commented, hoisting himself into the rear seat of the Jeep. "Shipping us out to Buck and intervening with social services saved our asses."

"Speak for yourself. I've always looked after my own ass." Dakota started the Jeep as Shawn swung onto the front seat.

"But you wouldn't have the skills or the ranch you can lay claim to now without Father Joe and Buck's interference," Shawn reminded him. Of the three of them, Dakota struggled the hardest with his past, and the unsolved murder of his mother that had landed him in foster care.

"True."

Shawn hid his smile. Dakota always used as few words as possible, as if it hurt to talk. He could be a mean son of a bitch if a situation warranted it, such as an injustice against a woman or animal, but Shawn and Clayton were probably the only two who knew just how supportive and caring he was with those who mattered to him.

Dakota dropped Shawn off first, and he bid them good night before entering his log cabin home. They each had built a place on the ranch but lived miles apart, Dakota having settled closest to the barns, stables, and bunkhouse, since he managed the ranch business. Like Shawn, Clayton opted to build closer to the main road into Mountain Bend, the small, revitalized mining town where they both worked. As the town's only prosecutor, Clayton often worked with him and the sheriff's department when preparing for a case.

Curly and Mo, the abandoned German shepherds he had recently adopted, greeted him with wagging tails, rubbing their still-too-thin bodies against his legs. "Hey, guys. Have you behaved?" He petted each one then tossed his hat on a hook by the door and left the entry to scan the main living, dining, and kitchen area for any destructive behavior. Other than a shredded magazine and one of his boots lying unharmed in front of the stone fireplace, it appeared the dogs were finally getting comfortable with his absences.

"Good boys," he praised them, walking into the kitchen to get them a treat from under the large, farmhouse sink.

Shawn wasn't much of a cook, but he still built a large kitchen with plenty of storage in the forest-green cabinets and prep space on the long butcher-block counters. Dark wood beams lined the vaulted ceiling across the entire space and matched the stain on the wood floors, a nice contrast to the lighter logs covering half the walls. The rest were painted the same dark green as the cabinets, but the south wall of windows allowed for bright rays of sunshine to lighten this portion of the house during most of the day.

"Okay, you two, out you go for a spell."

He let the dogs out the slider then pivoted, his eyes landing on the answering machine's blinking light. And here he'd just been thinking about Father Joe. The extra expense of keeping a landline just so the priest would stay in touch spoke to his deep affection for the man who had been there for him ever since the death of Shawn's father. He didn't need to listen to the message, as Father Joe was the only one who had the number to that phone. No one else of his acquaintance harbored such an aversion and ineptness toward the modern convenience of cell phones.

Pulling out his cell, he remained by the slider to keep an eye on the dogs while he returned the call. "Hey, Father. What's up?"

"Just checking in with you, son. How are you guys getting by without Buck?"

"We miss him, but we're fine. Work keeps us busy. Miss Betty stays in touch, and that helps." Shawn grinned, watching the dogs wrestle.

"If you'd find a nice girl and settle down, you'd be happier."

"How do you know?" he retorted but with humor. "You've never married."

"I'm married to the church, and she's made me happy." Father paused a moment then said in a guarded tone, "Are you seeing anyone?"

Wondering at the sudden interest in his love life,

Shawn said, "I *see* several women all the time. No one special, if that's what you're wondering. Why all this concern over my bachelorhood?"

"You just turned thirty-five. I figured you would be ready to think about having a family."

"I have a family. You, Dakota, and Clayton. And Miss Betty still likes to cook for us and give us hugs."

Unbidden, the memory of thin arms clinging to his neck and a small body quivering against his chest popped into his head. He still thought of that little girl now and then, wishing Father Joe would tell him more about where she ended up living after that night. Other than to tell Shawn he and social services had found another foster home for the girl, and that she was safe, the priest had refused to disclose any other information about her, including her name. For months after relocating to Buck's ranch, he had been plagued with thoughts and worry about the frail little girl, her trusting green eyes haunting him even in sleep. Shawn had no explanation for the strong impact that short encounter made on him to still remember her so vividly after all this time.

"That's good. I'll let you go, son. You take care, now."

"You too, Father." Shawn hung up, thinking that was one of the oddest conversations he'd ever had with the priest.

****

Lisa jerked as Master Wade snapped the flogger across her buttocks again, the spreader bar holding her feet apart and immobile, keeping her in position on the chain. Tears blurred the wall in front of her when the painful stinging the multiple strands elicited failed to bring her usual, much needed response of numbing relief. Fisting her cuffed hands above her, she braced for the next lash, praying for the temporary distraction she craved.

"What do you want, Lisa?" Master Wade demanded, running the thin leather strips over her clenched buttocks. Her bare body glistened with perspiration, but inside she remained cold.

"More, please. And...harder," she whispered, ashamed of the depth of her longing for this extreme method of escapism. When she'd first explored BDSM as a means to cope with the nightmares that had plagued her since childhood, she'd never dreamed she would need it to withstand with the possibility of a stalker intent on hurting her, or worse.

His low curse didn't bode well for her, but he struck again anyway, giving her the more forceful blow she'd begged for. Blistering heat erupted across her tender globes, wrenching a cry from her tight throat, but her mind remained aware of her surroundings in the Phoenix club, her pussy dry when she yearned for those blessed moments of freedom an orgasm offered.

Lisa whimpered and hung her head, her long hair falling forward to hide her face as Master Wade stepped close enough his leather vest and pants brushed her bare skin. When he bent to free her ankles, she knew the scene was over and disappointment swamped her.

"Your head isn't in the game tonight, Lisa," he admonished as he rose and released her bound wrists next.

She fell against him and sighed when his arms came around her. He was her favorite Dom, but even with him before tonight, she had continued to fall short of achieving her ultimate goal of exorcising her sexual hangups. Now, with the added fear and stress of having picked up a stalker, she couldn't even gain the minimal relief she used to reap from alternative sex before the first harassing phone call.

"I know. I'm sorry, sir."

Master Wade squeezed her then reached for her dress and panties lying on a chair against the wall. He slipped the sleeveless sheath over her head, and it fell to just above her knees, the soft, pale-blue cotton cool against her hot buttocks.

"I can do that, sir," she protested when he stooped down and held out her panties for her to step into.

"I know you can, but let me help you. It's the least I can do since I've failed to get you to tell me what's wrong."

Tears pricked Lisa's eyes again as she braced on his shoulders and lifted her feet one at a time. For over a year now she'd entrusted her body to Master Wade and a few others, seeking answers to a blurry past, and now, evasion from a personal threat. The small orgasmic pops she'd managed under their tutelage were the first and only bouts of pleasure she'd reaped from any sexual encounter. Granted, she could only boast of two affairs before seeking membership to the club, but neither her fondness for those men nor the sex had been enough to thaw the ice that formed whenever they touched her.

I can't tell you what I'm not sure about. Lisa

stepped away from Master Wade as he dropped his hands. "I'm sorry. If I knew, I would tell you." She looked around the large, converted warehouse at the people she'd come to know well enough to bare herself in front of, but still refrained from forming close friendships, determined to keep this part of her life secret. Most of their faces reflected the contentment and pleasure she wanted more than anything else except her safety. As much as she would miss this place, and those who understood why she came here, maybe it would be best if she stayed away for a while. Although, if whoever was targeting her made good on his threats, she wouldn't survive long enough to miss anything.

"I'll try harder next time, if you still want to scene with me," she told him.

"Of course." Taking her arm, he steered her toward the entrance. "But do yourself a favor and invest in some honest soul-searching before you return. You have to be honest with yourself before you can be totally open with any Dom. You're always welcome here, Lisa."

Master Wade kissed her, a soft brush of his lips that left her aching for the hard, masterful possession she knew he preferred. As she walked out the door he held open for her, she vowed not to return until she could earn his time and respect again. She wound her way through the packed parking lot toward the yellow Volkswagen she'd scrimped and saved for, slid behind the wheel and flipped on the AC. Early spring was still cool in most places, but in Arizona the temperatures were already soaring into the nineties. Before pulling onto the highway, she checked her phone, releasing her held breath when she saw no new texts or messages from the stranger intent on causing her grief. Even after she changed her number twice, he managed to find her.

His persistence scared the hell out of her.

Lisa shuddered, recalling a vague memory of the heavy weight and foul breath of another man the last time she experienced this kind of fear. The terror that man and her stalker instilled was different from the heart-wrenching uncertainty she could still remember from the night police had awoken her and taken her to a stranger's house, saying only that her mother wasn't coming home. It had taken weeks of counseling before she'd understood the finality of the car accident that had taken her mother's life as she'd driven home from work. Lisa had only been in that first foster home one week before being uprooted again and delivered into the hands of that now faceless man.

As always, whenever that foggy memory made an unwelcome return, a wave of anxiety caused her heartbeat to speed up, and her mind automatically pulled up a clearer image of smokey gray eyes filled with concern. Unlike the man who had frightened her that night, *his* face, voice, and comforting hold were easy to recall. Even now, all these years later, he was her go-to guy when she needed a good memory to divert her from her troubles. Knowing there was someone out there who had once found her worth saving always helped calm her rioting thoughts.

Approaching the city limits, Lisa attempted to apply the brakes, her heart jumping to her throat as the pedal went to the floor without slowing the car.

Gripping the wheel, she tried again to no avail and turned nauseous. *He's done threatening.* Her palms turned sweaty from her struggle with the wheel, and she racked her brain for options. Shaking inside and out, she spotted a flat grassy area up ahead, praying she survived the sudden jolt as she veered off the road before reaching to shut off the ignition.

She gasped as the seat belt dug into her shoulder and waist with the abrupt, jarring halt of the compact, fast-moving car. The sudden silence in the pitch-black surroundings scared her as much as the close call. She knew with gut-clenching certainty her brakes had been tampered with and who was responsible. He, whoever he was, was no longer content with tormenting phone messages.

As soon as she could pry her fingers loose from the steering wheel, she reached for her phone and called the tow service her insurance would pay for. Then she dialed the only person left whom she would trust with her life, her voice trembling with residual fear when he answered and she asked, "Father, can you come get me?"

****

"What's wrong, child?"

Father Joe's heart ached watching Lisa pace his living room, her face pale, hands still trembling from that near accident. He'd kept in touch with his children over the past twenty years, even though he'd known it wasn't wise to let himself become not only attached to her and the boys but invested in their lives. They might not have sprung from his body, but his close bond with his childhood friend, Patrick McDuff, had ensured his love and support of Patrick's son, Shawn, especially after Patrick's untimely death. When Shawn had showed up late that night all those years ago, bruised and carrying the traumatized child, there had been no turning any of them away.

"Something has been bothering you for a while now." He handed her a Coke, her favorite drink, and nodded toward the sofa. "Sit down and tell me."

She sank onto the couch and looked at him with haunted eyes, the same heartbreaking gaze she'd given him the night Shawn had rescued her from their abusive foster parent. One of his biggest regrets would always be not stepping in sooner to see that Shawn was placed in a decent home instead of trusting the system to do right by him.

Joe could tell from the three boys' faces they wouldn't stay put in another foster home, and he'd decided to take matters into his own hands. After putting a quick call in to a good friend of his, he'd contacted the authorities and had a "come to Jesus" talk about the children's safety. Between Lisa's traumatized state and Shawn's accounting of that night's events, they'd agreed to the relocation of the boys to Buck Cooper's ranch, and the family in his parish Joe knew well and had suggested for the young girl.

"Someone, I don't know who, has been leaving threatening messages on my phone and in texts. I've tried ignoring them, changing my number, and reporting the harassment, but that hasn't stopped him. And now, to-tonight..." Lisa sucked in a deep breath then took a long swallow of pop before continuing. "My brakes failed, Father, and I don't think it was due to mechanical error. They were fine driving earlier, and I just had my car in for a tune-up."

Joe went cold at the thought of someone so callously tormenting her. "We need to get a report from the shop that has your car now," he said, taking a seat on the chair facing the sofa then leaning forward to clasp his hands between his knees to hide his own shaking. "Then we can go to the police."

Lisa shook her head. "It won't do any good, not until I have proof the same person tampered with the car. They were little help when I contacted them about the calls. I'm scared enough, Father, that I think I should get out of Phoenix for a little while." She blinked back tears as she sipped her Coke again. Lowering the can, she pleaded with him for answers. "But where would I go, and how would I get away without whoever this is finding out?"

Shawn would keep her safe. Joe didn't doubt that for a second. But sending her to him would negate his efforts to help both of them get over that difficult night. After separating them twenty years ago, he'd sought professional advice on how to answer Shawn's constant questions about Lisa, thinking it best the two of them put that night behind them as fast as possible. The psychologist he'd talked to had agreed, suggesting letting Shawn know she was fine without relating any personal details. Dr. Forbes had assured him that nine times out of ten, children suffering a one-time abusive situation reached adulthood without difficulty or lingering side effects.

She'd been right, and Shawn had quit asking after Lisa within a few months of living in Idaho.

He'd kept in touch with Lisa's foster parents and her when she'd started attending the parish school. Like Shawn, she'd stopped asking about "that boy" after settling in her new home and getting comfortable with the other foster kids and her new environment, but the disappointment and sadness reflected on her small face whenever he'd answered her inquiries by telling her he had to go away still haunted him.

Lately, he'd wondered if he should have let them correspond. Who knew if they had connected in a special way that night, or could have developed a special friendship over the years if he hadn't kept them apart? It bothered him they were both still single, Lisa alone with no close friends and rarely dating, and Shawn, as well as Clayton and Dakota, showing no interest in settling down with families of their own.

Still, he hesitated to throw them together after all this time, worried about resurrecting bad memories. With Lisa's safety on the line, he chose to err on the side of caution and let fate decide the rest.

"I agree, you should relocate, at least for a while. Stay here tonight, give me time to come up with something. Will you do that?"

One thing he admired about Lisa was her independence, her refusal to lean on anyone, even if he thought a lot of it stemmed from fear of opening herself up for possible heartache. There were times he worried she used it as a shield to keep others from getting too close and then losing them, like her mother. She was careful, too careful not to let herself rely on anyone else for her happiness.

She hesitated, biting her lower lip before shaking her head. "No, I have a slew of papers to grade this weekend and don't want to impose on you other than to ask for a ride back to my apartment. I'm not sure leaving is even an option, as I have to work, but I could apply for a short leave, so it's something I've considered."

"You might think about a permanent move. You've never lived anywhere else, and a new location could open up all kinds of possibilities for your future, not to mention throwing off this stalker."

A teasing glint entered her eyes as a grin replaced her stressed look. "No matchmaking with one of your out-of-state friends, Father." She shook her finger at him as she stood then tossed her can in the recycle bin.

He laughed. "No, nothing like that, I promise. Come on, then, I'll take you home."

"Okay. Thank you. Maybe come morning, the mechanic will tell me my brakes were just worn, and I will have bothered you for nothing."

"We can only hope and pray the solution is that easy." Picking up his keys, he prayed she stayed safe. "With the new priest taking on the majority of work, I've cut down on my duties, so don't hesitate to call me if you need anything. I can be at your apartment in ten minutes."

"I will, I promise."

****

Lisa didn't sleep well. She tossed and turned all night, jumping at every sound, thinking it was an intruder. After taking a hot shower and downing three cups of coffee the next morning, she sat cross-legged on the floor and started grading a stack of papers, waiting for the call about her car. What would she do, where would she go if they confirmed her worst nightmare and found someone had tampered with the brakes? Her head was so muddled from lack of sleep and lingering trepidation from her close call last night, she couldn't even concentrate on her first-graders simple addition problems. Father Joe's suggestion to get away for a while had matched what she'd been thinking and warranted consideration, but she didn't have the finances to get by without working for long.

Rubbing her eyes an hour later, she jerked when her phone pealed and she recognized the repair shop's number. His report of a leak in her brake fluid caused nausea to churn in her cramped abdomen. She was meticulous about getting regular tune-ups, and even though he didn't say it, her gut instinct told her that leak didn't just happen, that somehow her stalker had sabotaged the line. That wasn't enough to take to the authorities, so she thanked him and hung up after saying she would pick up her repaired car before closing today.

Lisa spent the evening on pins and needles, wavering between risking the odds she would stay safe and being overly cautious by leaving town for a while. She had friends, but no one she was close to and could rely on for help other than Father Joe, but she hesitated to lean on the sixty-five-year-old priest too much. She also didn't want to worry him, not after all he'd done for her over the years, and had put off calling him with an update about her car long enough.

He answered on the first ring, and she felt bad for making him wait. "What did the mechanic say?" he asked.

"They found a leak in the brake fluid, a common enough occurrence to negate going to the cops again. Maybe I panicked for nothing." She didn't believe that but saw no need to stress Father Joe out more than she already had.

"Don't take the chance, Lisa." He paused a moment before his tone turned cautious as he asked, "Do you remember much about the night the three teenagers brought you here from your first foster home?"

The unexpected resurrection of that trauma-filled night made Lisa's knees give out, and she sank down onto the sofa with a painful indrawn breath. She didn't recall much about two of those boys, but she'd never completely forgotten the one with the soothing deep voice, comforting hold, and soft gray eyes, or the confusing heartache of his swift disappearance from her life. As a distressed, confused child, the pang of betrayal she experienced when he vanished without a word after sweeping in like a superhero to save her had made sense. As an adult twenty years later, she never expected the quick return of those hurt feelings just from bringing up that memory.

"Vaguely," she replied. "Why?"

"They live near Mountain Bend, Idaho, and I'm sure one would let you stay with him..."

"No, no way will I impose on strangers with my

problem," she interrupted, refusing to consider such a plan.

"One of them, Shawn McDuff, is a deputy sheriff. I know you'll be okay with him," Father Joe stated calmly, as if ready for her negative reaction.

Lisa couldn't imagine the humiliation of showing up on one of those men's doorsteps all these years later, the once pathetic girl now a grown woman still in need of protection from a cowardly bully. "I don't want to put someone out to deal with this, Father."

"I understand your reluctance, but I don't know what else to tell you. You can't go off alone, with no destination or plan for the next few weeks. Will you at least think about it tonight?"

Lisa rubbed her brow, hating she caused the worry in his voice. "Yes, I'll do that and call you in the morning," she agreed to ease his concern. "Thanks, Father."

She hung up and, unable to help herself, she padded over to her computer in the corner, curiosity overruling common sense. "This is stupid," she mumbled, sitting down and typing in a search for sheriff's deputies, Mountain Bend, Idaho. Then her heart tumbled as a picture popped up, and she eyed the rugged features of the badge-wearing cowboy named Shawn McDuff for a hint of recognition. A black Stetson shielded his eyes, but she could make out a straight nose, shadowed jawline, and sculpted lips curled up at the corners. Thick, muscled arms were crossed in front of a wide chest, and her mouth went dry as she tried to remember which one he was.

Scrolling down, she found a clipping from the Mountain Bend newspaper and read the accounting of his rescue of a four-year-old boy who had fallen down a well. *Twenty years and this one is still saving innocent kids.* Was he the one who had carried her to safety that night? The article continued on the next page, but it wasn't the photo of the grateful parents that snagged her attention. Right below the headline story was a large ad by the local school district, depicting their dire need for a substitute elementary teacher to finish the final school semester in the rural area.

Lisa shoved away from the computer and jumped to her feet. "What am I thinking? I can't pack up and move to Idaho for a few months." Pacing the worn carpet, she told herself it was an insane idea to contemplate leaving the only place she'd ever lived, and approaching one of those men was out of the question. She barely recalled the only one she'd gotten a good look at before he'd scooped her up in his arms, and, in all likelihood, they had forgotten all about her a long time ago. There was no way she'd impacted any of their lives as much as the one's timely intervention had hers. Spinning around, she shut the computer down and resumed grading, determined to put that idea out of her mind.

By the time she finished dinner Sunday evening and there were no more threatening messages, Lisa allowed the butterfly flutters of apprehension in her stomach to ease. Her relief lasted all of one hour before a loud thump against her door caused her to jump and her pulse to skitter as she walked over and looked out the peep hole. She didn't see anyone, only the taillights of a car speeding out of the apartment complex parking lot. Taking a deep, shaky breath, she inched open the door, gasping and stumbling back when her eyes landed on the dead cat lying in a pool of blood on the welcome mat, a note pinned to its shoulder.

YOU'RE NEXT.

Shaken, Lisa slammed and locked the door, then sank to the floor and sobbed into her hands. What had she ever done to deserve such hatred? She no longer cared if the idea of running away, leaving the only city she'd called home, caused her grief. This latest threat left her no choice but to get away as fast as possible. As soon as she got herself under control, she called Father Joe.

"Okay, Father," she said when he answered. "I agree, I need to leave for a while."

"What's happened, child?" he asked, his voice laced with concern.

She wasn't that lost, frightened child he'd first met anymore, but at that moment, the insecurities she remembered after her mother died came rushing to the surface in full force. Her tone wobbled as she described the poor cat, her heart continuing to pound against her chest.

"If he can do such a cruel thing, I have no doubt he's serious about hurting me. I can get hold of the principal tonight and request an emergency leave. Just promise me one thing, Father."

"Anything, if it will get you to agree to go to Idaho for a while."

"Don't let any of those men know I'm coming. Please. If I get that temporary position, two months' absence should be enough for him to lose interest in me."

He hesitated, and she held her breath, hoping he would agree. When he did, it was with obvious reluctance.

"Okay, but promise you'll contact me when you get there."

"I will, Father."

CHAPTER TWO

❝Have you given any more thought to running?" Lyle Fenton asked Shawn the minute he stepped inside the county office.

Placing his fists on his hips, Shawn sent his boss, the sheriff, an irritated look. "I just finished my shift, and you're already hounding me."

"Hey, time's wasting. You only have another week to put your name in. The election is just seven months away."

Shawn swept by Lyle and tossed his hat onto his desk, still unsure whether he wanted to get into the politics of law enforcement. Lyle planned to retire this year, and as the deputy sheriff with the most time under his belt, he supposed he was the logical person to take his place. Problem was, he'd been contemplating returning to ranching full-time, alongside Dakota, ever since an un-scratchable itch had taken up residence between his shoulder blades right before his thirty-fifth birthday. So far, he'd failed to find a reason for his discontent or a remedy to alleviate his recent dissatisfaction with life. He'd hoped buying Spurs would give him the extracurricular activity and up-kick he was craving. But the second-floor renovation was just completed and the grand opening planned for tonight, and he still found himself mired in a funk.

Kevin Holmes, the second-shift new hire, cast them a curious glance from his seat at the switchboard.

With a huff, Shawn faced Lyle again.

"I wouldn't be good at kissing ass, Lyle. You know that."

Lyle folded his tall, lanky frame into his chair behind his desk. His handlebar mustache twitched with the derisive curl of his mouth. "Trust me, I know. That doesn't negate the fact you'd be good at the job. In fact, I view your honesty and low tolerance for BS a point in your favor."

Shawn pulled out the tickets he'd written that day and tossed them to Kevin to log in on the computer. Other than breaking up a noon brawl at the Watering Hole, Mountain Bend's only bar, and answering yet another domestic disturbance call from the Campbell's neighbor, Gladys Archibald, his day had been uneventful. He still simmered with frustration over Louise Campbell's refusal to press charges against her abusive, good-for-nothing husband, Chester, but as he'd learned from all the other times he'd been called to the house, there was nothing he could do about it until she was ready to say she'd had enough.

"I've got a week, yet. Let me give it some more thought." He sat down to write up his daily report, ignoring Lyle's grunt, eager now to clock out and go for a long, vigorous ride on his dun Mustang, Nevada.

Thanks to daylight savings, the sun still shone bright when Shawn left the precinct and slid behind the wheel of his cruiser, the use of the sheriff's vehicle just one of the perks of working for the state. Mountain Bend was an eclectic blend of the old and new, tourists drawn to the nearby ghost town attraction along the river. The well-preserved original buildings dating back to the 1880s mining days were toured by thousands every year. Early travelers were already trickling in, as he noted by the full parking lot at the brewery steak house on the edge of town, and the no vacancy sign at the hotel.

Mountain Bend's small population of year-round residents almost doubled during the summer months, the extra revenue enough to see them through the long, cold winters when they had their town to themselves. The extra work meant a lot of overtime for the department and kept Shawn away from the ranch way too much during the nicest weather when he enjoyed being out on the land the most. Even so, he couldn't bring himself to walk away from the job he loved and used to reap such satisfaction from.

He hated his recent wishy-washy decision making and uncertainty, and hoped it was a temporary side effect of whatever was causing his discontent. Opting to take the rural, two-lane country road to the ranch, he took his time, well aware he was stalling before going out to Spurs. He wasn't in the mood for socializing but was obligated to show up for their new opening as an owner and to introduce the private rooms on the added second story to the members.

The view of snow-capped mountains rising behind widespread, soon-to-be-golden wheat fields settled any lingering tension from a busy day, and thankfully, today was no exception.

A mile out of town, he spotted a compact yellow car on the side of the road up ahead, a petite woman with shoulder-length white-blonde hair delivering a swift kick to the flat rear tire. A grin tugged at his lips as he pulled up behind the Volkswagen, wondering if her pale face was due to hurting her foot or her natural complexion. She swung her head toward him as he got out, and he was struck by a chord of familiarity even though he would swear he didn't know her.

Striding toward her, he saw a flash of surprise in her eyes as he nudged the brim of his Stetson up and quickly sought to reassure her. "Ma'am. I'm Deputy Sheriff McDuff. If you'll pop your trunk, I'll give you a hand."

"Oh, I...well, okay. Thank you."

She swallowed, and damn if he didn't want to put his mouth on that slender throat, sink his teeth into her soft skin. The instant flare of lust caught him off-guard, and was unacceptable. He'd stopped as an officer of the law sworn to look after others, not as a Dom drawn by her flustered appearance.

"No problem." Shawn forced himself to look away from her ass encased in snug denim as she pivoted and bent inside the open driver's-side door to pull the trunk lever. She straightened, tucking her hair behind her ear as she faced him again. Her striking green eyes held a hint of wariness, clinging to the sight of him as if he weren't real, that look tugging at his memory banks again even though he could swear he'd never met the woman. "Is there a problem, ma'am?" he asked, moving to lift out the spare, taking note of the packed trunk and rear seat. He should admonish her for blocking her view with belongings, but, given her state of apprehension and the compact size of the VW, he refrained.

"No." She shook her head and stepped away from him as he attached the jack. "I just didn't expect...I mean, there's been no traffic on this road."

"Yeah, it's used mostly by the ranchers, not travelers. Where are you headed?" He popped the flat tire off, eyeing the bald tread. It was a wonder she hadn't suffered this fate before today.

She peered up at him. "Mountain Bend. Am I close?"

Her gaze skittered off to the side, making him question why he made her nervous. The thought of a cop or anyone else giving her just cause for such uneasiness didn't sit well with him.

"About a mile, is all. You must have turned off the highway an exit too soon. That happens a lot. What brings you to Mountain Bend?" He hoped his casual chatter put her at ease. She was wound as tight as the raccoons when the dogs chased after them.

"A temporary job offer."

When she wasn't any more forthcoming, he nudged his hat back, swiveling on the balls of his feet toward the spare, and looked up at her again. "Not too many jobs that would entice an outsider..." Shawn snapped his fingers. "You must be the new teacher hired to fill in for Cathy Daniels." He was glad to see her narrow shoulders finally relax. While he was all for women who traveled alone practicing caution, he didn't care for the nervous tension pouring off her in waves. Too bad being a cop didn't give him the right to demand answers about the source of her obvious agitation.

"Yes. I'll finish teaching her second graders while

she's on maternity leave, and maybe stick around to fill in for summer school. I don't know yet."

She stooped and handed him a lug nut before he asked, a hint she knew how to change a flat. That's what he got for assuming she was too petite and delicate to handle the chore. He could still swear he knew her from somewhere, that he'd seen those eyes before, but for the life of him, he couldn't imagine where.

"Have we met?" he asked bluntly, not one to sit around and wonder for long. Her gaze widened, but she shook her head.

"This is the first time I've been to Idaho," she replied, shifting her eyes to the side again.

That wasn't really an answer, but Shawn let it go for now in favor of getting them both on their way. He tightened the last bolt in place, spun the tire, then pushed to his feet. "That should hold you until you can get it into the body shop for new tires. All four need to be replaced. Here."

After wiping his hands on the towel she handed him, he reached into his shirt pocket and withdrew one of his cards. Scrawling Ed's name and address on the back, he handed it to her, unprepared for the electric jolt that hit him when the tips of his fingers brushed hers. She gasped, jerking her hand back after taking the card, and he wondered if she experienced the same heat as he. He hadn't reacted so strongly to first meeting a woman in a long time, if ever, and wondered what the hell was wrong with him. He was a master at sexual control, but right now, all he could think about was bending her over the rounded hood of the VW and shoving those butt-hugging jeans down, baring her lily-white ass to play with while he plummeted her sweet pussy.

It was Shawn's turn to step away from her, that wild thought and the image it put in his head too distracting, not to mention ill-suited for the situation. Hell, he hadn't even asked her name. "Ed's the only mechanic in town, but a damn good one. He'll get you fixed up, Miss...?"

She hesitated before answering with her first direct look. "Halldor, Lisa. Thank you, Sheriff."

The name didn't ring any bells, and Shawn let it go, his interest obviously muddling his head. "Take the first right up the road and that will take you into Mountain Bend. Welcome to Idaho, Miss Halldor." With a farewell tip of his hat brim, he pivoted and returned to his cruiser. By the time he slid behind the wheel, she was driving past him with a wave, that wary expression still on her face.

****

Lisa gripped the steering wheel, glancing in the rear view mirror. She kept driving until she saw the last of Sheriff Shawn McDuff's taillights, then pulled over until she could calm her racing heart. Nothing could have prepared her for that unexpected encounter with the man she was sure had rescued her that night twenty years ago. She'd recognized him right away, not from the grainy newspaper photo but from the impact of looking into those piercing gray eyes again. Only this time, his astute gaze slammed into her with the same jarring force as the jolt of heated awareness that went through her when their hands touched. She floundered with uncertainty over how to deal with coming face-to-face with him again, and her unforeseen, adult reaction to that simple touch. The sexual longing he had reawakened inside her was even harder to understand.

When her application for the substitute teaching position was accepted hours after she'd submitted it, she'd given her principal the rundown on her situation and he hadn't hesitated to grant her a leave of absence until the fall. As she'd packed in a hurry to get away from whoever was out to get her, her only goal had been obtaining a sense of safety. Worse than the threatening phone calls from her stalker had been his silence the last few days before she'd gotten on the road with her car packed to the hilt. The last threat of the dead cat had scared her into moving quickly, whether she'd gotten the job or not.

Playing it safe, she had withdrawn enough money from her meager checking and savings accounts to pay cash for gas and lodging since leaving Arizona. Lisa doubted this person could get access to her credit card transactions and track her whereabouts, but she wasn't taking any chances after going to such extremes to get away from him. She'd counted on her sudden disappearance to discourage her stalker, and knowing her one-time rescuer would be close by had inadvertently helped her make the decision. She hadn't planned on meeting any of them and never imagined she would get hot and flustered from the light brush of her rescuer's fingers against hers and the penetrating astuteness of his eyes. The craving to submit to that focused gaze still trembled deep inside her, reminding her of the way she used to respond to the Doms at the club before becoming a victim had turned her cold inside.

I didn't move here for an affair. That thought had never entered in any of the talks she'd had with herself whenever common sense intruded and tried to change her mind about coming to Mountain Bend. The nagging voice that kept insisting this was a stupid idea was speaking loud and clear again as she resumed driving.

Despite her lingering stupor over that chance meeting, Lisa was well aware Shawn had shown no signs of recognizing her. She'd never expected any of them would, but admitting the one who mattered the most didn't help to quell the spark of arousal still warming her inside and out. By the time she reached the Mountain Bend city limits sign and mammoth welcome billboard, the hypersensitive nerve endings throughout her body had returned to normal. Too bad she couldn't say the same about the conflicting chaos still filling her head.

She was more grateful now than ever for Master Wade's written referral to Spurs, a nearby private club, that he'd given her before she'd left. At least she would have a venue to escape to when she needed relief from her taut nerves, or if she wanted to take her mind off the one man she had no business lusting after. With luck, the change of scene and Doms would be enough to break through the ice that had prevented her from responding ever since the first threatening phone call from a stranger had brought about a return of her childhood nightmares.

After living her whole life in Phoenix, the country's

fifth largest city, she'd assumed adjusting to life in such a small community would take some time. Instead, as she drove through town and spotted just one restaurant attached to a reconstructed brewery, three fast-food joints, and a two-street combined business and shopping district, she realized the conveniences were all a bike ride from several rental options.

Following the owner's directions, Lisa found the Miner's Junction Bed and Breakfast with no problem. Making reservations for a week at the quaint wood-planked, renovated nineteenth-century home seemed the fastest way to get here and then scout for a small temporary rental. The corner lot offered parking in the rear, and after grabbing her toiletries suitcase and purse, leaving her larger bags for later, she followed the sidewalk around to the front entrance. The rush of a gurgling river reached her ears, and she wondered how close it was to the established, tree-lined neighborhood.

Opening the ornate front door, she stepped inside where a dark-haired woman behind a short counter greeted her with a beaming smile. "Welcome to Miner's Junction. You must be Lisa."

"Yes. You're Ms. Zimmerman?" Lisa set her bag down and held out her hand.

"Jen, please. You'll learn quick enough we don't stand on formality around here. How was your trip?" Jen turned the register around for Lisa to sign.

"Good, other than taking the wrong exit off the highway. I found you, though, and the detour at least gave me a mini-tour of the countryside."

"Oh, you should have called. I could have driven

out to get you. It's easy to get turned around on our country roads and find yourself smack dab in the middle of one of the surrounding ranches. Not that any of our neighbors would mind. Well, maybe crotchety old man Sanders who owns the Bar S. I can see why he never married. He...oh, I'm sorry. I tend to ramble on. It's a good thing Drew isn't here, or he'd give me 'the look.'" She wiggled her fingers in a mime of quotation marks.

Lisa chuckled, enjoying Jen's sense of humor and envying the spark in her eyes when she mentioned her husband. She wished she could boast about someone special enough in her life to make her that happy. Instead, there was now someone who wanted to hurt her, or worse, and she couldn't even contemplate getting that close to anyone. She refused to let her current circumstances ruin her upbeat mood and picked up her bag as Jen grabbed a key off a pegboard and came around the counter.

"I don't mind you telling me about the people here. Anything you can share about the town will help me get acclimated to a new place. This is the first time I've lived anywhere except Phoenix." She hesitated as Jen turned toward the staircase that hugged the wall, then broached a touchy subject that needed clearing. "I appreciate you taking my reservation without a credit card to hold it."

Jen glanced at her with her hand on the bottom newel post of the staircase. "To be honest, there was something in your voice that prompted me to take that chance. Whatever you're fleeing from back home, I hope you'll find solace here. It's a great community."

Her astuteness reminded Lisa of Shawn's intense focus on her and the warm fuzzies his attention had generated. Given how much calmer and more relaxed she was already, maybe this escape would work out for her after all.

"I hope so, too, Jen."

****

By the end of her first week teaching in Mountain Bend, Lisa had discovered the vast, end-of-March weather difference between Arizona and Idaho. Back home, she could count on the temperature soaring into the upper eighties and low nineties during the onset of spring and start of the last term of school. Her classroom of eighteen second graders didn't seem to mind slipping on jackets before going outside for recess, but it had taken her the first few days to remember to remind them when they wanted to dash out the doors.

Going down the row where they were lined up at the door for dismissal, she made sure each little seven-year-old had his or her book bag and jacket before opening the door. "Have a good weekend," she said when the final bell rang.

"Bye, Ms. Halldor."

The chorus of farewells was followed by the thunder of small feet hitting the wide hallway from all the grade school classrooms at once. The middle and high schools were in separate buildings next to the elementary school, each class significantly smaller in number than the least populated grades in the Phoenix district. It hadn't taken Lisa long to get to know her students, or to discover the benefits of working with fewer kids.

She waited until she saw the last of them connect with a parent or designated pickup person out front before returning to her room. Watching the time, she straightened up the desks then filled her satchel with papers to grade before locking her desk drawers and turning off the lights. The staff had welcomed her on Monday, and she'd enjoyed lingering after school to visit and get to know them better in the last few days, but she didn't want to keep Jen waiting. Lisa was looking forward to moving into the vacant unit in the duplex Jen and Drew owned a few streets over from their bed and breakfast, and was grateful for the money renting it would save her.

Lisa waved goodbye to a few teachers as she walked out to the staff parking lot, the sun warming her face despite the upper fifties temperature she was still acclimating to. Her head was in the clouds, wondering if she'd be safe by the time she returned home in August, before the much colder months of winter, and she wasn't paying attention to others in the parking lot until a deep, amused voice startled her into jerking around to the right.

"Hello again."

With her heart thumping overtime, Lisa gazed at Shawn McDuff over the hood of her car. He regarded her with a quizzical expression, and her mouth went dry, her palms turning clammy as she took in the late-day bristles darkening his jawline and the tilt to his head. She couldn't help thinking about him this past week, recalling his potent stare, broad shoulders, and imposing height, and wishing she'd impacted his life as much as he had hers.

"Sorry. I didn't notice you. Hello, Sheriff." Lisa waved her hand toward the schools. "What brings you here?"

"Deputy Sheriff. A tussle between two high schoolers that revealed the pot they were fighting over. Their parents just picked them up." He strode around the car and reached past her to open her driver's side door, his thick forearm brushing her hip. Ignoring her hasty sidestep, he leaned on top of the open door and asked, "How are you liking it here?"

Lisa took a deep breath, forcing herself to get her act together. She'd never stuttered over a man before, and usually enjoyed getting to know new people. Even though they'd met before, they'd been so young, and it was such a long time ago, and under difficult circumstances. It was dumb to be hurt he didn't remember her, and likely not in her best interest if something she said or did reminded him. His stay in that foster home must have been longer, and worse than the few hours of her memory. She doubted he would appreciate the past showing up on his doorstep.

"I love it. Everyone has been so nice, and welcoming, but I really need to get going. I have an appointment to look at a rental."

Shawn nodded, stepping out of her way. "That would be the Zimmermans' place, right? I ran into Drew yesterday."

She stood close enough to glimpse his eyes under his hat, warming from his intense focus. "How did you know I was staying at their B&B?"

He shrugged. "I asked about you. You've made quite a change with your move from Arizona, Ms. Halldor."

Her shoulders went rigid at hearing that, the thought of someone, anyone, prying into her life rubbing her wrong after all the grief she'd suffered from picking up a crazed stalker. "Yes, well, sometimes change is good, or necessary. If you'll excuse me."

Shawn tipped his hat, his tone a shade rougher as he said, "I hope it's a good move for you. Get those tires replaced soon."

Lisa slid behind the wheel, her eyes following Shawn as he walked over to his cruiser. She bristled at his parting order then stifled her irritation. He wasn't privy to her low finances, at least she hoped his checking up on her hadn't gone that far. Between the travel expenses, staying at the B&B, and now the deposit and first month's rent she assumed Jen would ask for, her cash wouldn't stretch to include tires until she got paid next week.

Growing up in a big city hadn't prepared Lisa for the closeness of small-town living, and, in her haste to get away, she never thought about what she'd do if they came face-to-face again. She would either have to get a grip on her response every time she saw Shawn, or consider telling him where and when they'd met before.

Lisa hoped a new place with new Doms would help break through the block she'd suffered with the last few months but had planned to wait a little longer before visiting the private club, Spurs. But maybe she would go tonight and seek a distraction from thinking about Shawn. She wasn't sure what to expect when she met her anonymous childhood rescuer again, but it wasn't the instant heat conjuring up all kinds of hot fantasies that took her mind off the threats of a crazy person. It wouldn't do to let her guard down, even this far from home, despite feeling safer than she had in a long time.

****

What the hell was it about the new teacher that kept bugging him? Shawn waited until she drove away before heading back to the precinct, the wariness in her gaze still bothering him. That look in eyes the same emerald green as the little girl he'd carried out of Atkins' house was eerily similar, and he figured that was why she seemed so familiar. Unlike that much younger girl, Lisa didn't appear happy to see him the two times they'd met. Her frigid tone when he'd admitted prying into her life couldn't have conveyed her displeasure any better.

The flash of irritation that crossed her face just now and the kick she'd delivered to her flat tire last weekend revealed a quick temper lying beneath the soft-spoken cautiousness she portrayed. He wasn't sure what it meant admitting he enjoyed poking at her to ruffle her feathers, but she was a nice distraction from his recent moodiness.

"Monday is the deadline," Lyle announced the minute Shawn entered the office.

"I remember and plan to discuss it with Clayton and Dakota this weekend," he replied, crossing to his desk with a nod toward Andi, their dispatcher.

Shawn still hadn't decided whether or not to campaign for sheriff over the summer. He supposed he could toss his hat in and drop out if he didn't care for the politics that came with the job.

He scooped up a handful of sunflower seeds from the drawer as he sat down behind his desk. Lyle leaned a hip against the corner and said, "You're a better choice than Roberts or Sandusky."

"Thanks, but I have an obligation to the ranch to consider, and, right now, a report to write up." He gave his boss a pointed look, refusing to discuss the job further, and didn't want to hear any more compliments calculated to influence his decision.

"You're a stubborn son of a bitch," Lyle muttered.

"Funny, that's what Buck always said." Hearing the familiar gripe stated with a note of humor brought up the grief of losing the gruff rancher who had taken them in and made them a family.

"They don't come better than Cooper, that's for sure." Lyle straightened with a sigh. "I won't push you, but please give it some thought this weekend when you discuss it with the boys. Like I've said, there's no one I trust as much as you to fill my shoes."

"You could always stay on."

"Trust me, I've thought about it, if you don't run. Anyway, I'm headed out. Have a good weekend."

"You too, boss."

By the time Shawn finished his paperwork it was after five and he was eager to clear the cobwebs out of his head with a rigorous ride. Leaving the precinct, he walked next door to Clayton's office, surprised to find he'd already left for the day. Then he remembered that tonight potential new members could check out

Spurs for free, and the three of them were supposed to meet there early. He strode to his cruiser to head home, his enthusiasm for socializing at what used to be his favorite extracurricular activity still at a low. Clayton loved the law and holding lawbreakers accountable as much as he did arresting them for their criminal activity, but unlike him lately, both of his friends were happy to set work and their evening down time aside for time with a willing submissive.

After getting through their rebellious stage without the Coopers giving up on them, he, Clayton, and Dakota had left to attend college, remembering what it was like to be a victim. For Shawn, whose father had taught him to always stand up for the underdog, choosing a career in law enforcement had been easy. But he'd come to love the ranch just as much, which made it difficult to choose between the two. As deputy sheriff, he enjoyed more time off, fewer responsibilities, and less stress, leaving him able to work both jobs.

His thoughts switched gears as he drove by the spot where he'd changed Lisa Halldor's tire. Shawn didn't care for puzzles, and the tugs on his memory banks the schoolteacher kept prompting were bugging the heck out of him. If he didn't know better, he would think she was the same girl he'd rescued all those years ago. Since the odds of that were on par with winning the lottery, he discounted that possibility as soon as it popped up. Father Joe would have given him notice if that were the case. There's no way the priest had forgotten how he'd pestered him for information about the frail child who had clung to him with such trust.

As Shawn pulled in front of his home, Clayton drove up behind him in his Bronco, dashing his hopes of coming up with a work excuse to delay pulling his weight at the club. Sliding out of the cruiser, he gave himself a mental kick for the selfish idea and jerked a thumb toward the front door as Clayton joined him.

"Come on in. It won't take me long to get ready."

"We have time. I finished early today, but you were still out." A satisfied grin creased Clayton's tan face, revealing the dimples women loved. "Nailed the son of a bitch with a ten-year mandatory sentence. Fuck, but winning is good."

"I pity the poor person whose circumstances should grant them leniency but they end up with you on their case. You're a cold bastard in the courtroom."

Clayton possessed a ruthless, unforgiving streak when it came to lawbreakers. He'd never forgiven the courts for letting the drunk driver who had smashed into his parent's car, killing them instantly while leading the cops on a high-speed chase, walk free on a technicality. As a prosecutor, he never acknowledged gray areas by offering a plea bargain or reduced sentence.

His grin turned wicked as he replied, "I save my warm, good nature for those sweet submissives. They love me."

Shawn sent him a wry look as they entered the cabin. "Until you dump them. I thought I heard last week they have a bet going on regarding who can hold your attention the longest."

"Cool. I can have some fun with that. Don't you ever tire of all this wood?" he questioned, looking around the log walls and wood ceiling."

"Don't you ever tire of the industrial look?" Shawn didn't know what Clayton found appealing about open duct work and the modern iron and brick décor of his home.

"Can't say I do, not yet, anyway. Hey, there. You going to let me pet you today?" Clayton squatted down and held a hand out to the dogs as they rose from their beds but stayed out of reach.

"Mo, Curly, come." Shawn patted his leg but the shepherds didn't budge. "Sorry, Clay. There are dog treats under the sink. Try bribing them while I change."

While taking a quick shower, Shawn made an effort to get in the mood to pull his weight as co-owner of Spurs tonight. That meant taking the time to socialize with new guests, show them around or give a demonstration or two, and at least act like he enjoyed exerting his dominance. It pissed him off to find himself so blasé about indulging his sexual preferences at this age. Thirty-five wasn't even close to fifty, when he'd expected to go through the recent up-and-down mood swings plaguing him. Both Clayton and Dakota had passed their mid-thirties birthday, and neither seemed bothered.

After dressing in his usual club attire of jeans, boots, and a black leather vest over a cream work shirt with the sleeves rolled up to his elbows, he was in a marginally better frame of mind. His attitude improved even more when he returned to the living area and saw the dogs had made friendly with Clayton.

"Was it your charm or a treat?"

"My charm, of course. But the large dog biscuits

didn't hurt my case."

"I'll bet. I need to let them out for a bit before we leave, so we have time to eat."

Clayton winced with exaggeration. "Nothing you put together, I hope."

"No," he returned, unoffended. He was the first to admit he couldn't cook worth a damn. "I picked up barbeque."

"Works for me. I'll put it in while you keep an eye on the dogs."

An hour later, Shawn drove to Spurs, determined to get his head back in the game of playing and off everything else for the night.

CHAPTER THREE

L isa didn't have as much trouble finding the tucked-away, log-hewn private club as she did finding a place to park. She was used to a smaller venue and, seeing so many vehicles, she almost whipped around and returned to her newly rented home. The thought of spending another lonely evening by herself held less appeal than hanging out in such a large crowd, though, and she found a space big enough for her compact car at the far end of the last row.

No one else was arriving as she made her way to the front door, but it was already close to the ten o'clock deadline to enter, according to the website information for guest night. Besides shoring up her nerve to not only try a new place but to give the lifestyle another shot at breaking through the mental block holding back her physical response, moving from the B&B into the rental house had taken longer than she'd anticipated.

Fatigue tugged at her as she entered, and she questioned whether she should have waited another night to seek a Dom willing to take her on for the few months she would be here. Her unplanned-for encounters with Shawn had overcome the relief from putting distance between her and her stalker with plaguing thoughts and dreams of a deep need she couldn't label. Attraction or lust didn't seem to cover the extent of her reaction the two times they'd come across each other, leaving her both befuddled and annoyed. This was not what she'd anticipated when coming here, but then, her main concern had centered around getting away to someplace safe, so she had that excuse to rely on.

A young brunette wearing a red satin teddy that barely covered her full breasts greeted Lisa from behind a desk. "Hello. Welcome to Spurs. You've just made it as Master Dakota sent instructions to lock the doors." She stood, coming around the desk with a smile, wearing the shortest denim cutoffs Lisa had ever seen with a pair of red cowgirl boots. The odd ensemble somehow suited the hostess who looked to be not older than nineteen or twenty. "I'm Charlotte. Go ahead and sign the roster while I lock the doors. I don't want to get on Master Dakota's bad side."

Lisa returned her grin, remembering a few Doms she'd steered clear of at her other club to avoid their reputed strict punishments after learning how much she could take and still reap benefits. While the relief she'd gotten through pain-induced stimulation had surprised her, and she'd pushed one Master into more, it was Master Wade who helped her understand, and accept that the harsher aspects of the lifestyle weren't for her. He had taken her to the very edge of her limit, so good at his craft he knew when to stop before she did, and scolded her for pressuring him for more. She shuddered, recalling his alternative means for punishment.

There were only eleven names above hers on the list of guests, which, given the parking lot, surprised her. "What's the N next to some of these names?"

she asked Charlotte when the receptionist returned to the desk.

"It stands for newbie, and it's also on their nametag. What brings you here tonight, the free admission, or are you new to Boise?"

"New to Mountain Bend. I've taken a temporary job, for now."

"Awesome. Your timing is perfect. The new owners have just completed a second story addition, and we're all pleased with the private rooms and loft lounge. Come on. I'll see which Master is free to show you around, since I'm assuming you don't need instructions on the standard club rules."

"No, only those specific to this club."

Lisa followed her through the double doors, taking in the row of Stetsons hanging on hooks along the wall. "Oh, wow, no wonder the parking lot is full. This place is huge."

"It's even bigger with the upper levels." Charlotte pointed to the right where a staircase led to a hallway that ran the length of the building in front of five closed doors. At wood and wrought iron railing ran along both upper levels. "It looks like they're already in use – otherwise the doors are left open."

With a nod, Lisa's gaze swept the center of the room's rafter-and-skylighted ceiling, shifting to glimpse the seating on the upper opposite side before taking in the lower floor. She wasn't a connoisseur of country western music, but the two-stepping dancers gyrating their hips in tune to an upbeat song matched the rhythm with an ease she envied, considering what a klutz she was on the dance floor. Different bondage apparatus were positioned along the side walls, and, from what she could see across the huge room and out the windows, opportunities to indulge outdoors were also provided. All of the stools around the circular, center-positioned bar were occupied and about half of the tables.

"You like?" Charlotte asked.

"What? Oh, yes, sorry. Just taking in the differences and similarities to the club I was a member of back home." Nervously, Lisa ran her hands down her short denim skirt, comparing her sleeveless white blouse covering a blue demi bra to the sexy lingerie most of the women were wearing. "I wasn't sure what to wear, as I planned to just check the place and Masters out tonight."

"You're fine. As long as there's bare skin, they're happy. You're in luck." Charlotte nodded toward the tall, bald man approaching them dressed in black leathers and vest, his chest bare, a gold earring winking under the dim lighting, and his dark eyes zeroed in on Lisa. "It seems Master Simon is up next to chaperone. Good evening, Sir."

"Charlotte, sweetheart, introduce me to our guest, please."

The deep rumble of his voice reminded Lisa of Shawn's tone when he had addressed her, Master Simon's focused gaze much the same also. Or maybe she was still thinking too much about him, even though she wouldn't mind getting to know this Master better.

"This is Lisa Halldor, sir. She's new to Mountain Bend, but not to the lifestyle. Lisa, I hope you enjoy your evening and come back."

Master Simon nodded, giving Charlotte permission

to leave before holding his hand out to Lisa. "Would you prefer to start with a tour or to visit over a drink?"

She took his hand, and when she didn't get even a spark, her hopes of diluting her unexpected ache for Shawn were dashed. Refusing to give up, she worked up a smile and replied, "We can talk while walking around, can't we?"

"You like to use your time efficiently, an admirable trait. All right, then, let's start with a stroll down the south side."

Lisa went with him, leaning close and craning her head up to hear better as they viewed scenes already in progress, and he introduced her to other members along the way. She told him which equipment she had experience with, as well as her preferences. He didn't pressure her for information, which made him easy to talk to, and his strong hold of her hand kept her grounded, a familiar and welcome feeling she'd missed lately. She warmed when he stopped at a spanking bench on the north side where the bound woman's bright red butt was on an elevated display.

"It appears Kathie has been up to her usual antics," Master Simon drawled. "Lisa, this is Master Clayton. What did she do this time to earn your displeasure, Clayton?"

Master Clayton delivered a blistering swat with his wooden paddle before turning to face them. Lisa expected to see him scowling, his face etched with displeasure at the woman, but his lips were twitching and his blue eyes twinkling. His sandy hair curled around his neck, contrasting with his tanned, rugged face and dark jawline.

"She tried to trip me to get my attention off one of our guests." He jerked a thumb toward the girl seated on a cushion at the foot of the bench. "Alicia here is getting educated on what happens when a sub steps out of line, which this one" – he caressed Kathie's abused butt – "likes to do. Welcome to Spurs, Lisa."

She forced her eyes away from the casual stroking of his hand over the puffy cheeks and the damp sheen coating the submissive's swollen folds. "Thank you, sir."

"You enjoy setting Kathie straight just as much," Master Simon said. "You two make a good pair." His smirk drew Lisa's curiosity until his friend answered.

"For the occasional hook up, sure."

Ah, that was it – Master Clayton stuck with playing the field. She would keep him in mind if she decided to join. She liked the way he maintained his easy going attitude while meting out harsh discipline.

"Later, then." As Master Simon tugged her into moving, she reddened from both men's eyes shifting to the obvious outline of her hardened nipples. Leaning down, he asked, "Are you interested in stepping the evening up a notch?"

Yes, the scene, and Kathie's obvious response to the pain, had reminded her how she would get wet and aroused before she'd shut down. "Honestly, sir, I'm not sure." Between thoughts of Shawn continuing to distract her and worrying about a return of the coldness that had recently nixed the few rewards she'd reaped from submission, she wanted to be careful about not making a mistake going forward.

"Do you want to tell me what's holding you back? You've indicated you have experience."

"I'm being cautious is all. The last few times, I haven't...there are some upheavals in my life that... oh, hell, I don't know what I want to say." Lisa blew out a frustrated breath and tried to pull out of his grip.

Master Simon refused to let her, instead drawing her against his leather-clad legs and bare chest. She sucked in a breath, the quick flare of arousal from his control offering a sliver of hope. "Running doesn't solve problems, it only delays them. You came tonight for a reason. Why not see it through? Unless you have a preferred safeword, use the standard red, and I stop, no harm done. I know the signs of stress to watch for, Lisa."

Because she really wanted to, Lisa agreed before she changed her mind. "Yes, sir, I'd like that, but I prefer facing you."

"Agreed. I would have insisted anyway as that makes my job easier. How about a chain station." He pointed several feet down. "One just came available. You don't mind public scenes, right?"

She liked he wanted to make sure, even though she was experienced. Oddly enough, exhibitionism had turned her on from the onset of her foray into BDSM, giving her a big boost of courage those first few times. "Right, and the chain station is fine."

He ushered her past a metal contraption with an assortment of narrow pads. She shivered, recognizing the restraining bench most often used by those into S&M. A thrill of anticipation tickled her skin as they reached the chain and he attached the cuffs, raising her arms before his hands went to the buttons of her blouse.

"We'll start with partial undress since this is a new venue for you. Pretty," he said, releasing the last button and spreading her top to reveal her propped-up breasts in the strapless bra.

Lisa shuffled her bare feet, enjoying his praise, but the exposure to cooler air and a few interested gazes made her more than ready to get started. She clenched her hands as he flicked open the front clasp on the bra and removed it, her nipples puckering into even tighter nubs under his appreciative look and from the brush of his finger across each one that added a sizzle to her blood flow.

"Sir." She arched toward him in a silent plea, the need for a distraction from her woes rising to the surface of her insecurities.

"Relax, sweetheart, we'll get there. Which instrument do you prefer?"

He stepped back and twirled his finger for her to pivot and look behind her. His accommodating manner was starting to grate, and Lisa turned, wishing he would just take over. One of the things she liked best about submitting was letting a Dom take the weight of decision-making off her shoulders.

The array of pain-inflicting choices was familiar, and she chose her favorite. "The flogger, please, sir."

Lisa faced the room again as Master Simon picked a multi strand one with a short handle. He was a handsome man, his crooked smile when he stood in front of her again softening his otherwise chiseled face. Shawn's face popped into her head, the memory of the probing glint in his silver eyes and straightforward way of talking to her causing her pulse to flutter. She closed her eyes in order to concentrate on the man she was with and what he could hopefully do for her.

She shook as he trailed the thin strands across her quivering breasts then over her abdomen above the waistband of her skirt. Craving the sting, she held her breath, waiting for it. He continued to tease, tickling down the front of her legs then up her back and over her tense shoulders. A groan slipped past her compressed lips when he started over, taking the same path.

"Sir, please," she whimpered as he reached her breasts for the third time yet still denied her the bite of pain she craved.

"You're too impatient. It's been a while, you said. Open your eyes and enjoy the play."

She didn't want to; she only needed the ounce of relief she used to gain from this. It hadn't been much of a bump-up from the disappointments that had driven her to explore the lifestyle, but the orgasms she had experienced at the Doms' hands in Phoenix were more than she'd ever gotten from her vanilla affairs.

Used to obeying, she looked at him and replied, "I prefer a harder touch. Sir."

He sighed, as if let down, but nodded. Quaking with anticipation, she braced for the first snap, but when he struck her waist, the quick there-and-gone burn dwindled so fast she barely felt it. He was still treating her with kid gloves, adding to her disappointment and mounting frustration. Lisa bit her lip to keep from complaining, breathed in through her nose, and forced herself to be patient.

****

"This is ridiculous. Let me go, you jerk!"

Shawn narrowed his eyes and reached for the girl's bound wrist attached to the headboard slat. "If you just wanted to fuck a stranger, you've come to the wrong place."

This, *she* was why he hated newbie night. It was just his luck to pair up with an immature, annoying chit who had insisted on exploring her "needs" in one of the private rooms only to have her turn on him the second she realized he wasn't one of her college boys to lead around by his dick.

As soon as the cuff fell away and she lowered her arm, she slid the thin strap of her tank top down, lifting her breast out with a cajoling smile as she sat up. "Don't get so huffy just because I want both my hands free to touch you." She eyed him as if he were a decadent dessert.

"Candy, is it?" he asked politely, just to annoy her since he knew her name.

"With a K and an i, yes."

He barely refrained from rolling his eyes and almost laughed at her obvious struggle to keep from griping again. "I said you would be given a pass at several rules tonight, but whatever made you think you could use me, or any other member of our club, to add a kinky notch to your dorm-room bed? Get up, and I'll escort you out."

Kandi jumped off the bed, tossed her head in disdain, and glared at him. "You can't speak for other people. I want to hang out for a while."

She likely had in mind to show him what he was

missing by turning her down. He was almost tempted to let her have her way. It would be funny to watch her humiliating failure, but he had neither the time nor the patience to mess with her any longer.

"Wrong, I *can* speak for any member or guest in *my* club." Shawn jerked a thumb toward the door. "Out. Now."

She flounced by him with an exaggerated huff, and he followed her out to the second-floor landing and down to the stairs wishing he could keep on going once he saw her to her car. He doubted Clayton and Dakota, or any of the other Doms assisting with the membership activities, would appreciate him dodging his responsibilities. Until he figured out what was driving his sulky moods of late, he would have to suck it up and do his part, even if his heart wasn't in it.

Shawn waited until Kandi with a K and an i drove off before returning inside and heading to the bar. A cold beer would go down real nice about now. He stopped to say a few words to patrons along the way while scanning the room to see who was doing what and with whom. Even though the three of them knew the members well and trusted them, it was always good to keep an eye out for a potential problem.

He came to a sudden halt as his gaze zeroed in on the blonde at a chain station, his body jerking in stunned surprise seeing Lisa bound in his club. The somewhat evasive schoolteacher hadn't projected any submissive vibes the two times they'd met, but looking at her face etched with discouragement, her slim body and soft breasts arching forward in silent supplication, there was no denying she'd found something she needed by indulging in alternate sex at least once before. Simon, a Dom he knew well, seemed to temper the stroke of his flogger as he aimed for the fleshy undercurve of one breast.

Shawn frowned as Lisa opened her eyes, and, even from this distance, he could see the frustrated ache reflected in the green depths. That undisguised longing added to the questions crowding his head about the last woman he expected to see here, the woman he couldn't stop thinking about. As obsessed and confused about her as he'd been since their first encounter, he hadn't dared to imagine her bound and naked, succumbing to his control.

As puzzled by Simon's uncharacteristic restraint, given Lisa's clear body language, as he was by his slightly miffed feelings toward the other man, he veered their way. As if sensing his approach, her gaze flew toward him, rounding in disbelief, her breasts rising with her startled gasp.

Without taking his eyes off hers, Shawn asked, "Master Simon, would you mind if I have a word with this guest?"

"Not at all, since she's not happy with me."

Lisa winced. "Oh, but I am, sir. I'm sorry, I was just hoping..." She paused in consternation, looking away from both men.

Simon used the flogger handle to lift her chin and turn her face up to his. "You were hoping for a fast scene, some quick burns to distract you from whatever is on your mind, and a just-as-fast orgasm, right?"

Lisa shuffled her feet and clenched her hands, her face turning pink under their unrelenting gazes as her jaw tightened. "If you're so good at reading people, why did you stall?"

He raised an arrogant brow. "My scene, my way. Master Shawn, let me know if you need me to return."

"Will do, thanks." Shawn nodded, grateful for Simon's insight. He should have known Simon wasn't oblivious to Lisa's needs.

He waited until they were as alone as they could be in a room holding over seventy people before giving Lisa his full attention. Taking in the damp ends of her hair clinging to her neck, he stepped close enough for her nipples to brush his chest. "I'm usually a pretty good judge of character, but gotta admit I never pictured you here at Spurs, Ms. Halldor." He smirked when she narrowed her eyes at the sarcastic inflection he'd used in saying her name.

"Then we're even, Deputy McDuff, since I never imagined you here, either. If you'll release me, please, I'll be on my way."

Oh, no, he wasn't letting her off that easy, not while gripped with the urge to erase the prim façade that replaced the stark desire she'd exhibited a moment ago by giving her what she'd come here seeking. Testing her, and himself, he slid his hands behind her neck then spread his fingers as he pushed them up under her hair to cradle her head in his palms. Watching the pulse jump in her neck, he could almost hear the rapid pounding of her heart.

"Not yet, and here, it's Master Shawn. You don't want to leave with your body still vibrating for the touch that will ease the strain from whatever is bothering you, do you? No, keep your eyes on me," he insisted when her attempt to pull free of his hold ended with that telltale shifting of her gaze, leaving no doubt she knew of her inability to shield her emotions.

"You want to continue with me? Are you sure?" she asked.

"Yes."

He found himself wanting to appease her straining needs as much as he needed answers about this constant tug of vague recognition. Again, he discounted the possibility she was the young girl he'd rescued so long ago despite the same coloring and soft voice that kept triggering the memory. That much coincidence was too farfetched to believe.

Shawn waited until her desire overrode her caution and she gave him a reluctant nod to continue. "Good, girl." He was never stingy with his praise when warranted. Dropping his hands to her shoulders, he caved to the temptation to touch her and drew his palms down her chest and over her nipples to cup the soft mounds. "So dainty, much like the rest of you. But you're tough on the inside, aren't you, Lisa?"

"When I need to be, Sir." She bit her lip as he squeezed her breasts before releasing them.

"Let me assure you that you don't need to be tonight, not with me. Let go whenever you're ready." Turning away, he walked to the wall of implements and chose a flogger with three short, wide straps and returned to stand behind her. "Do you wish to keep your skirt on?" he asked, snapping the strands on the back of her right thigh just below the hem.

A groan slipped past her compressed lips, a shudder rippling down her smooth back. "On, please."

Her slight hesitation told him she was tempted to reveal more of her body, and, with it, her needs, but he wouldn't push her past her comfort zone. Not until he knew more about her, not only where and when they'd connected before, but about what was causing the stress that drove her here tonight. As a new teacher in a small town, she should be aware of the risk to her reputation and job if the wrong person saw her here. Not that something like that had ever been a problem since he, Clayton, and Dakota had been members, or that they would care if it had. But, as sexist as it sounded, women were always held to a different moral standard, and, as an educator of young children, she was walking a very narrow line.

Shawn tickled the red marks on her thigh with the ends of the flogger, liking the way she shivered at the light touch on top of the lingering burn. With a flick of his wrist, he snapped the strands against her other thigh, leaving matching red stripes behind.

"How long have you been involved in the lifestyle?" he asked with a strike to her lower back.

"Not long. A little over a year. *Oh God.*" Lisa arched her back into his next swat, this one a little higher.

"What you don't reveal in words, you say in body language. That can work for now in here, Lisa, but not outside these doors." Shawn teased her by caressing his way up to her shoulders before drawing back and delivering two rapid slashes to the lily white soft skin.

"We don't..." Turning her head to look at him, she said, "Outside these doors, my life is no one's business. Sir."

Shawn moved to stand in front of her, her head

following him. "As long as you're not in trouble, I can respect that. If I discover otherwise, I *will* make your life my business."

Her eyes flashed with anger, but she held her tongue, he assumed in favor of finishing this scene.

****

Closing her eyes, Lisa set her worry over that vow aside and braced for the slice of prickly pain as Master Shawn lifted his arm. If he hadn't moved so close to her, so fast, allowed her to lean against that rock-hard body and look into the concern in those pewter eyes, she would have demanded her release and run away from the shocking revelation of his presence. She wasn't prepared to see him in this club, his eyes hot on her bare breasts, his broad shoulders rigid with the same disbelief that had clouded her thinking, or for the comforting security of his unbreakable hold.

She cried out with the hot sting of leather hitting her breast, the lovely burn it left behind making a beeline straight down to her pussy. The sudden, startling return of her response shook her, adding to her confusion over her conflicting feelings toward a man she barely knew. As much as she welcomed the slow build-up of arousal his takeover of this scene initiated, it didn't bode well for her to keep her distance from either Master Shawn or Deputy Sheriff McDuff. She was still working her way through the hurt his lack of memory produced, an unexpected emotion he didn't deserve the blame for.

Gathering all her wayward, unexplainable thoughts

together, she shoved them aside, determined to hold onto the pleasant euphoria slowly taking over her senses, just like she remembered before coldness had seeped in to take over. Master Shawn treated her other breast to a searing stroke, her sheath spasming in quick response to the pain.

"I prefer your eyes open and on me, Lisa."

Unable to help herself, she obeyed, even though she was more comfortable with her shields in place. She should have remembered that was almost impossible in private clubs such as this, and in front of such astute Doms.

"Better. Since you're cooperating nicely, I'll give you permission to close them again as long as you show me those pretty green eyes the second I insist."

Right now, with her body vibrating as close to normal for her as she could recall, she'd agree to anything. With a nod, she lowered her lids, his deep, commanding voice washing through her with his growled reprimand.

"Verbal answers, Lisa."

"Yes, sir." She thrilled to his willingness to alter strictness with leniency as he saw fit, even if she found his accuracy in reading her bothersome.

Stars lit up the blackness behind her closed eyes as fiery pain engulfed her right nipple with the next strike. His accurate aim had centered on the tender bud and left it throbbing in tune with the pulsations rippling along her vaginal walls. The low murmur of nearby voices fell away as she arched forward for the next blow, turning her torso just enough to entice a similar aim toward her other nipple.

Master Shawn didn't leave her aching, treating

that tip to the same blistering heat as she quaked in the restraints, praying for the one strike that would free her from months of disappointments.

"Tell me," he whispered seductively close to her ear, "have you ever climaxed from breast play?"

His warm breath in her ear upped her arousal another notch, along with the light brush of a calloused finger over one tormented nipple. "No, sir." Her heart sank at that admission and the odds of achieving the bliss of a mind-enveloping orgasm tonight despite the dampness coating her thong.

"Let's see what I can do about that, shall we?"

He didn't wait for an answer. Instead, she heard the flogger drop as he dipped his head to draw a turgid tip into his hot, suckling mouth. Lisa cried out at the strong pull on her sore nipple, and the sparks of pleasure the enhanced discomfort produced. She swayed closer to his bristled face, keeping her eyes sealed. The scrape of his whiskered cheek and jaw against her sensitive flesh added to the burning need throbbing between her legs, an ache she kept praying would burst into a wildfire.

Master Shawn took his time gnawing, sucking, and licking her nipple, one second intensifying the lingering pain, the next soothing it. One hand held her breast up for his mouth, the other reaching under her skirt to palm her bare buttock. The press of his long fingers into her soft flesh, so close to her aching, empty pussy, made her quiver with a longing she dared not succumb to at this point, not with the secret of who she was standing between them.

"Sir, please," she pled on a groan, hoping the tiny fluctuations starting in her pussy would continue toward an orgasm.

"Please what?" he asked, releasing her nipple and sliding to the other side. "Torment you some more? Okay."

To Lisa's astonishment, all it took to topple her over that climatic edge was the tight clamp of his mouth around her other nipple coinciding with the deep kneading of her buttock he initiated. Basking in the pain-induced, unexpected pop of pleasure, she flung her head back and sobbed with the release of pressure even though it was still less than what she'd achieved before she shut down. She didn't know how long she basked in her breakthrough and the ripples of warm undulations spreading up her core and through her straining body before her head cleared enough to realize he'd returned his hands to cup her skull and his insistent voice registered.

"Open your eyes, Lisa."

Remembering his instructions, she blinked until his tanned face came into focus, shivering from the cool air drying her still-quivering, perspiration-damp body. "S-sorry, I..." She blew out a breath and opened her mouth to start again, but he stopped her with a quick, somewhat chaste kiss.

"Don't apologize for letting go, Lisa." Holding her face up, he subjected her to a close scrutiny before nodding, apparently satisfied with whatever he saw. "Excellent. Get ready for me to release your arms."

She knew what he meant and held her breath for the tingling of blood rushing downward, eliciting tiny pinpricks as he lowered her hands to her sides. Releasing her breath on a *whoosh*, she fell against him with one more shudder. He held her without words, giving her time to get herself together. When she was tempted to linger, she pulled away, ready to leave and sort through the night's revelations by herself.

"Thank you, Master Shawn, but I really must get going now."

Shoving her hands aside as she reached to button her top, his closed face didn't reveal a clue as to his thoughts. "Next time, you'll do better for me. I'll walk you out after you put my number in your phone so you can get hold of me if you have trouble driving home."

Lisa wanted to argue about his confident assertion and assumption there would be a next time, but that would only delay her departure, and the sooner she got her head on straight about where to go from here with him, the better.

Shawn didn't want her to take off without seeking more answers, but he was learning to read her accurately, and her shuttered expression and tight jaw meant he'd pushed her enough tonight. Handing her her bra, he clasped her elbow and led her into the foyer.

"Tell me we haven't met before," he demanded, using his sternest Dom voice as they stepped outside. She tried to draw back, but he refused to loosen his hold. In a perverse way, he got a kick out of watching the wheels turn behind those emerald eyes as she whipped her head up, floundering over what to say.

Her attractive, smooth face hardened, and regret kicked him in the gut one second before she answered, "If you're so sure we've met before, when you come up with when or where, tell me, and we'll both be enlightened. I'm parked at the very end."

Shawn waited until he'd seen the last of Lisa's taillights before returning inside, chafing from unappeased curiosity and an engorged cock. He could still hear her whimpering cry upon climax, the way it had rung with a variety of pent-up emotions despite the signals it wasn't exactly a mind-blowing orgasm. The needy glaze still lingering in her eyes raised his protective instincts along with his lust. There was no denying he wanted the petite schoolteacher, or the fact she was hiding something, and he wondered if it was the reason she'd accepted a temporary, out-of-state job.

Dakota swiveled on the barstool as he approached, eyeing him with a raised dark brow as he took the seat next to him. "Did a newbie rub you wrong?"

"Why?"

"Because the look on your face is one I'm usually accused of, and I don't like the competition."

Shawn grinned, his tense muscles relaxing as he lifted a finger to their bartender, Ben, for a beer. It was always good to see Dakota's rare sense of humor make an appearance.

"Yeah, but not in the way you're thinking. She wasn't new to the lifestyle but not real experienced, either. I put a dent in some block holding her back, but not much, and only physically. The girl has secrets that are bugging me." Not to mention that nagging sense of having met her somewhere before.

Dakota shrugged and took a long pull of his brew before replying, "Next time, push her harder."

"That's your style, not mine. And you drive away

more than you hang on to, so I think I'll muddle my way past her defenses my way. Thanks, Ben." Shawn nodded to the Parks and Wildlife ranger whose only concession to indoor work was the two weekend nights he tended bar here at Spurs.

"Suit yourself, but my way is easier, and less taxing."

Ben smirked, having heard enough to get the gist of their conversation. "Your size alone intimidates even the not-so-timid ones, let alone that cold shoulder you like to fake subs out with."

"Look at that. Ben's got your number already, and he's only known you a fraction of the time Clayton and I have." Shawn gave Ben a thumbs up, ignoring Dakota's scowl as he stood.

"Bite me, both of you."

Dakota stalked off, but Shawn knew he wasn't pissed. His friend could take it as well as he dished it out. "I guess I better circulate and make sure all our new guests are taken care of, unless you want a break."

"No, I'm good. I'll take time to play once I send out the last call, but thanks." Ben lifted a hand as he turned to stroll to the waiting customers at the other end of the bar.

Shawn had lost his appetite to socialize or seek another partner to scene with, but he slid off the stool and forced himself to fulfill his obligation to his friends and now partners in this venue. He, Clayton, and Dakota hadn't let each other down in the twenty years since they'd met. He wouldn't start now just because a woman had managed to get under his skin for the first time.

CHAPTER FOUR

Paradise Valley, Arizona

"Did you find her?"

Bruce Pomeroy bristled with resentment as his father gave him his standard greeting the minute he walked in the door. "No, not yet," he replied tersely, frustrated with his search and the fact he'd lost track of the little bitch when he'd been so close to ridding himself of her pesky presence on Earth.

The old man's shoulders drooped, and he spun his wheelchair around on the marble entry floor. "Bring me a whiskey, will you, Son?"

Of course, Dad, anything to make you *happy.* He held back a curse and followed him into the high-ceiled great room, going to the corner bar while his dad wheeled over to the fireplace to brood. The day had been long and tedious, spent searching for Lisa Halldor again. He couldn't risk hiring a private detective even though he'd told the old man he was working with one. It wasn't the first lie he'd given his parent, and certainly not the worst. Not that he cared.

For twenty-four years, he'd suffered from learning his philandering father had sired a daughter, and he had a half-sister who was already five when he discovered her existence. His mother had turned a deaf ear to the news, much like she'd turned a blind eye to her husband's affairs over the years. The lifestyle from his millions was enough compensation for her. Since his father was away more than home during the first twenty years of Bruce's life, was it any wonder he'd taken after her and put maintaining his lavish lifestyle as his top priority?

Since his mother's assumption she would out live Frank due to their twenty-five-year age difference didn't pan out, Bruce had been looking forward to spending all those millions himself until his father fell for some religious nonsense. Surprise and anger didn't begin to cover his reaction when the old man announced he wanted to claim the daughter whose existence he'd ignored for twenty-nine years and make up for his neglect by adding her to his will. The only good news he'd given Bruce that day several weeks ago had been putting him in charge of locating her.

"You're not trying hard enough. Fire that investigator and find someone else," Frank demanded, his age-spotted hand shaking as he took the Waterford cut-crystal glass Bruce handed him. "How hard can it be? We know her name."

"It wouldn't make a difference. My guy is good, but if there are no leads, then it doesn't matter who you go with. She's not anywhere in the Phoenix area, but she'll surface somewhere." At least he hoped that proved true. There's the possibility his failed attempt to take her out with the faulty brakes had scared her enough to send her into hiding for good. If so, that would work as well in his favor as making sure she didn't live longer than dear old dad. He regretted letting his irritation push him into tormenting her with anonymous threats before seeing her dead.

"It's a nice evening. Let's sit outside until dinner," Bruce suggested, needing to keep on his good side.

"You go ahead." Frank waved his arm in a shooing motion.

Bruce refilled his drink, spun on his heel, and went out the French doors. Settling in a patio chair, he took a big, fiery gulp of whiskey, working to get his pissed-off frustration under control. His gaze skipped across the rippling clear water of the infinity pool to take in the majestic view their hilltop mansion offered, a reminder of what money could buy. Paradise Valley sat nestled in the foothills of Mummy Mountain with the Camelback and Piestewa Mountains hovering in the background and was home to only the wealthiest people in the state. Then there was his mounting gambling debt to consider, and the people he owed a small fortune to who didn't like to be kept waiting for payment.

He intended to remain one of the elite and get out from under his crushing debt by ensuring he stayed the sole heir to the Pomeroy fortune, and Bruce always got what he wanted.

****

Shawn leaned sideways as his dun Mustang, Nevada, made a sharp right to cut off the Black Angus from darting farther away from the herd. The stallion had been a handful to break in but worth every bruise and now loved riding. Spending the weekends on the range with Clayton, Dakota, and the ranch hands always helped to clear his head of cobwebs and plaguing thoughts, like one emerald-eyed blonde who was driving him nuts. The more time he spent with Lisa Halldor, the more she intrigued him, and the deeper his suspicions went that he knew her from somewhere.

He couldn't discount the significance of the flashbacks to that time in the past he'd thought he had put behind him, nor could he talk himself into believing in such a coincidence as she was the same girl he'd rescued so long ago. Unlike Clayton and Dakota, both of whom still struggled with the fact the people responsible for their parent's deaths hadn't paid the price for their crimes, Shawn was content knowing the armed domestic abuser who had shot and killed his father was still sitting in prison, serving a life sentence. With the help of Father Joe, he'd come to terms with his father's death, and even though he still missed him, he'd moved on from that hurtful time, honoring his father's memory by following his footsteps into law enforcement.

At least, he'd thought he'd adjusted well until he met Lisa and all he could think about was the night they'd fled the Atkins' house. And that made no sense.

"Good boy," Shawn praised Nevada with a pat on his neck as he straightened in the saddle and guided the Angus toward the herd grazing around the lake.

Wildflowers were starting to bud across the pasture, another sign of spring on top of the warmer weather. His biggest adjustment in moving from Arizona to Idaho had been the drastic climate differences – the winters here were damn cold and long. Still, after testing Buck's authority the first six months, he'd acclimated to the weather and his new life on the ranch with a spurt of enthusiasm.

"What are you thinking about that caused that shit-eating grin?" Clayton asked as he rode up on his tan, white-and-black quarter horse, Sierra.

"Buck, and how hard we tried to get him to send us back home at first. Christ but we were little bastards, weren't we?"

"Hell yeah. I thought for sure he'd beat the tar out of us when he caught us smoking in the horse barn ten minutes after finding us in the hayloft of the feed building and lecturing about the risk of fire. Man, he was livid. Ah, good times." Clayton sighed with feigned drama.

"We found out quick he had other ways to punish." Shawn winced as they rode. "Every muscle hurt the next day after he made us stay up all night scrubbing down each stall with soap and water. And we still had to go to school and do chores afterward."

"At least he caved and let us have the cherry pie Miss Betty made us. That helped."

"Her cooking always soothed our ruffled feathers," Shawn agreed, eyeing Dakota's scowl as he joined them, his head turned to watch the approach of a ranger's cruiser. "Huh, wonder what they're coming all the way out here for."

Ben Wilkins, their part-time bartender and a full-time ranger pulled to a stop and got out, leaning one arm on the open door. His Stetson shielded the upper half of his face, but there was no mistaking the tight set to his mouth that indicated trouble.

"What's up, Ben?" Shawn dismounted, along with Clayton, and the two of them walked toward Ben. Dakota remained on Phantom, his dappled-gray

Morgan.

"You've heard grizzlies have returned to the state, right?"

"Last year, yes, after what, a century of close to extirpation? I just read the oldest one on record, thirty-four years old, was found living in Yellowstone last month. Why?" Clayton asked.

"Because one a lot younger attacked a hunter. He's been air-ambulanced from the north into Boise. We're out spreading the word but wanted to give you guys the heads-up since the attack was so close to you. Watch your backs until we get him."

"Need help?" Dakota asked.

Shawn looked up at him as he rode closer, the stern set to his face revealing the concern he would never reveal in words.

"Not yet, but thanks, Dakota." Ben rubbed his jaw, shaking his head. "He must be just plain mean because the attack came out of nowhere, without provocation."

"So says the victim, right?" Shawn had arrested more than his share of abusive hunters who got their kicks out of torturing or killing for the sake of killing instead of for the sport and then the meat.

Ben nodded. "His testimony is all we have to go on right now, and, as of yet, no one has found cause not to believe him. If he's lying, he's paying a hefty price for whatever he tried with this bear. He's lucky to have survived."

"Appreciate the warning." Clayton dipped his head and turned back to his mount, saying over his shoulder, "We'll let you know if we spot him."

"Thanks, guys. Take care."

Shawn swung up onto Nevada, cursing over yet one more thing to worry about. He could tell by Ben's face his friend was as aware as he if a story about a grizzly attack got out, every big game hunter in the country would make a beeline for their state to make a name for himself. The sheriff's office had enough on their plate without that added headache, and he knew the park rangers were also overworked once hunting season opened.

"Relax, McDuff," Dakota drawled, managing his huge, spirited stallion with ease. "Attacks like that are rare, and between me and the hands, we can ensure the safety of our livestock. You won't need to change your schedule to watch over us."

Clayton chuckled at Shawn's frown. "It's true. You've got that look on your face."

They ribbed him a lot, claiming he was an overbearing ass whenever there was a threat floating around. Was it his fault he'd inherited a strong protective gene from his dad? Lisa's face popped into his head, her evasive looks and the worry often reflected in her eyes both hints she was carrying baggage of some kind. Was that why he couldn't quit thinking about her, was so intent on solving the riddle of who she was, where they'd met before? *Fuck*, probably.

"I've known neither of you needed someone to cover your backs since we were teens, but there's always safety in numbers. Remember that, Dakota. If you're good here, I'll ride back in. I have things to do yet today."

"Any of them have to do with the attractive blonde with the pretty breasts from last night?"

Clayton always did go for blunt questions when poking his nose into his or Dakota's business.

"Blonde? Was she the one who got under your skin last night?" Dakota asked with a sharp glance toward Shawn.

"No one got under my skin, it's just Clayton making an ass of himself, again. I'm grilling tonight if either of you wants to join me." Lifting his hand in a wave, Shawn turned Nevada toward the east and kicked him into a gallop.

There was nothing as exhilarating as tearing across a wide-open range with the wind whipping at your face and your body in tune with your steed's ground-eating strides. As much as he enjoyed the rigorous ride, Shawn arrived at the stables still debating over what step, if any, to take next with Lisa. On top of finding her attractive, she tempted him as a Dom to explore her submissive side further, and to get to the root of her problem. Her wary, reserved eyes with hints of trouble tugged at his protective instincts and whatever secret she was holding close that demanded investigating. The combination couldn't have been gift-wrapped and left on his doorstep in a more enticing package, and he figured the only solution was to get to know her better and earn her trust.

He couldn't rely on random meetings to accomplish that goal in the relatively short time she would be here, and certainly not at the club where emotions and libidos ran so high. Assuming she would agree, Shawn decided to ask her out. As soon as he learned where they'd met before, he was sure his odd obsession would disappear as fast as it came about.

It would have to, he determined as he tethered Nevada at a corral rail outside the horse barn. Given she was only in town for a few months, nothing long term could come of whatever relationship he could talk her into.

Satisfied with his decision, and confident of the outcome, he groomed Nevada and turned him out to pasture before hopping in his SUV and returning to his place to see what he had to go with the buffalo burgers.

****

Lisa jerked awake on a gasp, struggling to breathe, her hand on her constricted throat. Heart pounding in terror, she cast a frantic look around the dark room, trying to get her bearings. *Another dream, that's all.* That realization was little comfort as she sat up on the side of her bed, still shaking inside and out from the too-real heavy pressure threatening to suffocate her.

Reaching for the lamp next to the bed, she switched it on, wishing like hell the circumstances of why Shawn had whisked her out of that foster home had never resurrected again. Sometime between settling in with her new foster family and getting counseling, she'd effectively blocked most of the fear of that large, foul-breathed man pinning her to the bed, choosing to dwell on the comfort of strong arms and a deep, soothing voice instead. For the first time since her mother never returned home, a stranger had been willing to let her choose a path forward.

That night, with her assailant lying on the floor still

way too close, it had been a no-brainer to go with Shawn. She'd lived with the memory of that rescue without fear until the threatening phone calls had started, reviving the terror of being victimized. The first time she went to the club after getting that first scary message, she couldn't get past the coldness that had invaded her body. No matter how hard or what Master Wade tried, nothing had worked to separate her mind from her body, or to release the block keeping her from responding.

Just like twenty years ago, it was Shawn who had carried her out of the frigid darkness into the warm light. That didn't mean she wanted him to know who she was, or why she'd come to Mountain Bend. Despite that unreasonable pang when he didn't remember her, she wasn't about to let him think she'd come seeking his protection again.

Oh, and by the way, I'm in trouble again, so can you please help me?

Yeah, right.

Lisa pushed to her feet and padded down the short hall, nudging up the heat and turning on lights on her way to the kitchen. As she fixed a cup of hot tea, she relived every moment under Master Shawn's command at Spurs, the welcoming sting of his lashes, the hot clasp of his mouth on her nipples, and the strong, suckling pulls on her sore tips that had broken through her mental resistance. By the time the tea was ready, she was already warmer, pressing her thighs together as her thoughts resulted in a damp release from her empty pussy.

Before meeting her rescuer, she hadn't contemplated sex in months, too on edge over everything else even to miss the act. But now, with the dredges of another nightmare still hovering, she could really go for a bout of fucking that would take command not only of her body but her mind, enough to banish the lingering fear.

And that, more than anything else, told her how deeply meeting Shawn face-to-face again had affected her in such a short time. Other than safety from her stalker until he backed off, there was nothing for her here in Idaho, with him. She needed to remember any interest he showed in her came from the questions she had avoided answering, and now, from discovering her submissive interests. She couldn't bear to see his attentiveness change to suspicion were she to remind him of where he'd seen her before. In hindsight, she realized it was a mistake not to tell him about Father Joe and admit right away who she was. She blamed that error in judgment on the weeks of stress and fear clouding her mind and the surprise of their sudden meeting. As much as she craved another scene with the one man she now trusted above all others with her body, it might be best if she didn't push her luck by seeking him out at Spurs again.

Lisa couldn't get back to sleep, so she finished her weekend grading, cleaned the little bungalow that was the perfect size for her, and then took a long shower before accepting Jen's offer to drop in for breakfast and a visit at the B&B.

There was only one car in the guest lot behind Jen's place, but several were parked along the street. Lisa knew the Miner's Junction Sunday buffet was open to the public, offering a full menu, including Jen's specialty egg casserole and homemade cinnamon rolls.

"You're up early," Jen greeted her from behind the buffet table as Lisa walked into the dining room.

Picking up a plate, Lisa returned her smile. "Too early, but I couldn't get back to sleep. I hate buffets. They tempt me to take too much."

Jen eyed the scoop of scrambled eggs, bacon, sausage, and now hash browns she put on her plate. "I'm glad your aversion isn't stopping you. Leaning over the warming dishes, she whispered, "You and our hot deputy sheriff, huh?"

Lisa cursed her fair skin as heat spread over her face, her surprise at Jen's knowledge of where and with whom she'd spent Friday evening rendering her speechless for a moment. Jen's chuckle loosened her tongue.

"How did you find out?" she murmured, conscious of the diners seated behind her.

"Relax. Drew and I have been members for several years. Only a few people in Mountain Bend visit that club. Most regular goers are from Boise or neighboring ranches, like Shawn."

He owns a ranch? How much more didn't she know about him? Adding a roll to her plate, she replied, "I didn't see you there."

Jen handed her a napkin-rolled fork and knife as Lisa reached the end of the hot dishes and pondered the salad choices. "We came in late, and you left right after your scene. God, what I wouldn't give to have Master Shawn look at me like that even though my Drew is all I want."

Uncomfortable with her wrong assumption, Lisa

shook her head, juggling the plate and utensils to pick up a bowl of fruit. "I'm sure he treats all women, in and out of the club, the same. He's a nice guy."

"Nice?" Jen's grin spread into a wide smile, her eyes sparkling with amusement. "Yes, he is nice, but I sure wouldn't want to get on his bad side at Spurs. He is sexually dominant through and through, and overprotective to the point of bossiness with people he cares about. He's dumped several women who didn't take his concerns for their welfare seriously. One after her stupidity landed her in a bad scene when she thought to retaliate against Shawn's orders by hooking up with a new Dom who was still on probation with the former owner, Master Randy. Man, that was a nasty altercation between the three of them. Here, take this corner table."

Jen came around and led Lisa to a small, round table with two chairs next to the bay window overlooking the manicured back lawn. The morning sun splashed across the white-draped tablecloth and warmed Lisa's shoulders as she took a seat with her back to the windows.

Curiosity got the better of her, and she gestured to the other chair before Jen took off. "Can you sit a minute and tell me more? What happened to that Dom?" She couldn't imagine Shawn letting the guy off the hook with a warning if he broke club protocol.

"Sure. I just have to keep an eye on the food so it doesn't run low. As you can see, the buffet is popular on Sundays." Taking the empty chair, she leaned forward and said, "We were there and saw Shawn wrench the jerk's arm back when he went to swing his crop again after he'd just broken her skin. I've never seen him so mad, and it took Masters Randy and Clayton to pull him back."

Lisa shuddered and reached for the glass of ice water. She liked the bite of pain since she had discovered her heated response. At the time, she would have accepted anything that heightened her arousal, but imagining such excruciating agony left her cold. Not many could tolerate that kind of agony.

"What about the girl? Was he that pissed with her?" She munched on a piece of crispy bacon, unable to picture Shawn losing his temper with a woman, no matter what she'd done.

"Oh, he was just as furious, but like I said, he's one of the good guys. He gave her a verbal set-down, and Randy hustled her away." Jen sat back with a small shrug. "She hasn't returned. That's all I know. Shawn has a good reputation as deputy sheriff, strict but fair, and doesn't hesitate when someone needs help. You're lucky. He normally sticks to regular players, those he knows well. I can think of a few who will want to ask you what your secret is."

"I don't have a secret." Lisa didn't mean to snap at her, and realized how guilty she sounded. That's what she got for keeping her reason for taking the temporary teaching job to herself. "Sorry," she muttered. Jen cocked her head and gave her a quizzical look, and Lisa knew she needed to say something. "He stepped in when I was about to end the scene with Master Simon, and" – she spread her hands – "just took over. So, you see, I didn't do anything. It was all him."

"He must have seen something was off between you and Master Simon, then. He never hesitates to get involved if he thinks he needs to. Was that the case? Did he succeed?"

"More or less, and yes, better than anyone else anyway." She stopped short of revealing the whole truth, that she still had a ways to go before she could admit she was completely rid of the coldness. She wondered if she would have to be sure her stalker had lost interest in her for that to happen.

Lisa's second of her nine-week teaching job went as well as her first, but getting to know the students and staff better made her wish she could stay longer. She already knew she would miss Chelsea, the quiet, shy girl who reminded her of herself in grade school. Kim Delaney, the physical-education teacher, and Debra Devore, the fourth-grade teacher, were housemates, and had invited her for dinner Wednesday evening and to a movie in Boise this weekend. Since everyone else was married, Lisa appreciated their invitations, and hanging with them helped take her mind off Shawn and whether to risk returning to Spurs.

Until the closing bell rang on Thursday, and she saw him standing in her doorway. Her heart executed a slow roll, the odd sensation different from the immediate rush of blood through her veins. Leaning against the door jamb, crossed arms emphasizing his thick, corded muscles, his khaki law enforcement shirt stretched taut over his wide shoulders, and his lowered Stetson adding mystery to his face, who the heck wouldn't have such a strong reaction?

Chad, the red-haired trouble-maker of the class rushed over to Shawn without permission. Lisa pushed to her feet, her throat going dry, her pulse leaping as Shawn turned a crooked grin upon the boy. She cursed that quick response, wishing she could stay detached from his charm.

"Hey, Deputy McDuff. Are you gonna arrest somebody?"

"Chad, please return to your seat and wait to get in line like you're supposed to do," she admonished lightly, walking to the door.

"I'm already here, so I'm first."

"Chad." Shawn's deep rumble accompanied his hands falling to the little boy's shoulders. Turning him around, he said, "Do as Ms. Halldor instructed. Setting a good example is important."

"Fine, but I wanna watch you cuff 'em, so wait for me."

Shawn shook his head, removing his hat and nodding to Lisa. "I'm here to visit with your teacher, not to arrest anyone."

"Aw, shucks," Chad grumbled, shuffling his feet back to his desk.

Lisa looked up at Shawn in surprise, itching to sink her fingers into his thick, dark-brown hair where it curled around his neck. She stayed a safe foot away from him as the students lined up, but that didn't keep a small kernel of longing from forming, whether for the man or what he could do for her, she wasn't sure.

"What can I help you with, Deputy Sheriff?" She was proud of her steady voice, so at odds with her quivering abdominal muscles.

"It can wait until you've seen your students off." Moving out of the door, he made room for the kids to file past him, greeting several by name.

As she followed her students out, her arm brushed

against his, the simple contact enough to deliver an electric jolt of awareness and put a dent in her already scorched defenses. He was still waiting by her classroom door when she returned from walking the kids out to the buses and waiting parents. Lisa squared her shoulders, determined to stick with common sense and not cave to her physical needs.

Before she could say anything, he followed her into the classroom and closed the door behind him. "We're alone now, so you can drop the formalities. You're good with the kids."

"How do you know?" she asked, moving to her desk.

"I watched you the last fifteen minutes or so of class." Undeterred by her less than enthusiastic response to his sudden appearance, he came forward and hitched a hip against the desk, his hat dangling from one hand as he scraped his other hand through his hair, just like she wanted to do. "You don't need to worry about rumors of your attendance at Spurs getting out. This is a close-knit community, and despite the fast travel of gossip, those at the club respect other members' privacy. If they don't, they're out."

"I'm not officially a member, and I won't be here long enough to be considered part of the community. Besides, who says I'm worried?" She feigned nonchalance, but his comment did stir up a ripple of anxiety. That was something she'd never had to consider while living in Phoenix due to the sheer size of the city.

Shawn's deep chuckle vibrated down her spine as he reached out and gripped her chin. "You're easy to read, Lisa. For instance, I can tell you're not happy to see me. Why?"

She pulled out of his hold, his rough calluses brushing her chin, reminding her of the way he'd scraped across her sensitive nipples. Instead of answering, she asked again, "What brings you here, Deputy?"

His mouth curved in a sexy "I've got your number" hint. "Thursday is prime rib night at the brewery steak house. I'd like you to have dinner with me."

Lisa caught herself before she stumbled back in surprise, his invitation for a casual date something she hadn't expected. As much as an informal evening out appealed to her, it was the strong tug of that lure that made her pause, that and her growing infatuation with the man she only knew as her childhood rescuer.

"Considering my temporary stay in town, that's probably not a good idea, but I appreciate the offer."

"So polite," he murmured, those sharp eyes never leaving her face. "And troubled." Leaning over the desk, he cupped her nape and drew her forward until his mouth hovered above hers. "It's dinner, Lisa, not a marriage proposal. We both have to eat, and, unless you plan to stay away from Spurs during the next two months, I want to get to know you better before I restrain you again."

And just like that, her pussy spasmed with dampness, and she craved the hard pressure of his mouth taking hers. She opened her mouth without knowing what she was going to say then laughter from the hallway reminded her where they were, and she pulled away instead, putting space between them that did nothing to quell the neediness his presence stirred up.

"I'll pick you up at six." Shawn pivoted and strode to the door, saying without turning around, "I've got your address."

Flummoxed, Lisa stared after him. "How the heck did he do that? And why did I let him?" She couldn't help the flutter of anticipation skating through her, wondering if it was just their brief past or a stronger reason for her consuming interest in him.

****

"It's nice to see you again, Deputy Sheriff." The perky brunette greeted them as they entered the restaurant, her eyes devouring him as if he were on the menu.

"You, too, Tiffany. A table for two, please." He usually ignored the girl's harmless flirtations but didn't care for the cool look she gave Lisa.

Shawn removed his hat and laid a hand on Lisa's lower back as they followed the waitress to a table. Lisa's calf-length skirt swirled around her bare legs as she walked, the lime-green blouse a soft contrast to the dark denim. Her muscles tightened under his palm, but she didn't shift away from his touch despite the guarded look that hadn't left her face since she opened her door to him. The dim lighting in the restaurant wasn't enough to disguise the shadows in her eyes that hinted at secrets and plaguing thoughts she'd thus far refused to share.

He couldn't appease his curiosity and concern without answers, regardless of her continued evasions. Buck had taught them to meet challenges head on, and he hadn't walked away from one since. That spark of defiance in her eyes she tried hard to suppress whenever he pushed her buttons never failed to get a rise out of his cock, a nice perk that went with his uplifted spirits since meeting her.

"Thank you." Shawn nodded to Tiffany, taking the menus she handed him with a girlish blush.

"What can I get you to drink, Deputy Sheriff?" The quick glance she gave Lisa wasn't as friendly.

"I'll have a whiskey and Seven. Lisa?"

"A large Coke, please."

"Be right back." Tiffany spun around with a suggestive smile at Shawn.

Lisa regarded him with amusement as he sat down, one slim brow quirking. "Is she even out of high school?"

"Started college last fall, so no worries there if I was interested, which I'm not. I prefer women to girls, especially those who aren't timid about exploring alternatives to meet needs left unfulfilled." Handing her a menu across the candlelit table, he asked, "How long did it take you to try a private club as opposed to vanilla sex?"

"A few years and two failed relationships. Do you know everyone in town?" she asked without pause, smoothly changing the subject. She opened her menu and lifted it up between them, but Shawn saw through her attempt to hide her expressive face.

"Just about. I moved here twenty years ago. Did you grow up in Arizona?" Reaching across the table, he pushed her menu down and watched her brows dip in a frown as her eyes snapped up to his face.

"Better. I like looking at you when we talk."

Shawn could all but see the wheels turning in Lisa's head as she formed her answer, indecision swirling in the green depths of her gaze. The look of resignation crossing her face as she answered puzzled him.

"I don't recall living anywhere else. What do you recommend?"

"That you accompany me to Spurs tomorrow night," he tossed out to throw her off her game of steering the conversation away from her. After checking her out and learning she hailed from the same state as he, his suspicion they'd met before had increased.

Her sigh conveyed irritation. "I meant from the menu, and I already have plans."

"I know what you meant, but I wanted to see your reaction, and how hard you would try to come up with an excuse to turn me down even though you not only want to but need what I can give you. If you don't want the prime rib, which you won't find better, try the orange-glazed chicken. Saturday night works just as well. You're welcome to go early with me, or you can meet me there."

Tiffany returned as Lisa opened her mouth to reply, so instead, she thrust her menu at the girl. "I'll have the prime rib special. Thank you."

"I already know you want the special, Deputy Sheriff." She gave him a warm smile while not sparing a glance toward Lisa as she set the drinks in front of them.

Shawn frowned at her, handing over his menu. "Yes, and, Tiffany, please show more courtesy to my guest."

"Oh, of course, I'll get that for you, ma'am." She trounced off, looking flustered and embarrassed at his set-down.

"She called me ma'am on purpose. I'm only twenty-nine," Lisa grumbled.

That made her about the same age as the little girl he'd rescued would be, and he could no longer discount the possibility. If she was that same girl, odds were the trauma had kept her from remembering much about that night, at least not enough about him to jog her memory. If she did remember, he couldn't think of a reason for her not to say so. He needed to talk to Father Joe.

"You'll get over it. I lived in Phoenix until I was fifteen," he said, watching her closely. "It's bigger every time I return for a visit."

Lisa started to say something, seemed to change her mind as she took a drink of coke, then blurted, "I can meet you there Saturday."

Whatever decision she'd come to that brought about her agreement, he hoped she planned to share it with him this weekend. In the meantime, he would talk to Father Joe. Lifting his drink, he nodded.

"I'll look forward to it."

CHAPTER FIVE

What was I thinking? Oh, yeah, I wasn't *thinking straight, that was it.* Lisa shook her head at the mental conversation going on in her head, trying to find a way out of the corner she'd backed herself into with Shawn. She slammed the drawer shut on the bedroom dresser and sank onto the bed with a sigh of frustration. Telling herself she should have come clean with him from the very start wouldn't help now. The suspicion on his face the other night after she'd let slip with her age, added to his already probing questions, had sealed her fate.

She was royally screwed.

Worse than wondering how she was now going to tell him where he knew her from, and dreading his reaction, was how much she longed to meet him at Spurs tonight, like they'd arranged. The mere mention of having his attention focused on her had sent a wave of heated longing through her. The chance for another escape from her troubles proved too tempting to turn down, prompting her to accept his invitation. She planned to bring up that long ago night afterward, provided she could get up the nerve and steel herself against his displeasure.

The stress of keeping that secret was too much to continue juggling with her growing need for his ability to break through the coldness where others had failed. Her stalker had robbed her of the one outlet it had taken years to find that helped her escape the memory of that childhood trauma. She wanted that relief and ultimate enjoyment back but couldn't, in good conscience, keep Shawn in the dark about their association after tonight.

Lisa blew out a breath, the decision made as she rose to look through the clothes she'd brought from home one more time for something suitable to wear. Last week, she'd known guests would get a pass on attire, but Doms liked access to bare skin, lots and lots of bare skin. She didn't have a problem with nudity, admitting she enjoyed exhibitionism. The combined vulnerability of nakedness and bondage helped take her out of herself to that comfortable plateau where nothing mattered except the pleasure/ pain sweeping her body.

God, how she craved to reach that pinnacle again.

She hadn't heard from her stalker since leaving Arizona. She'd changed her number again right before taking off, but that hadn't stopped him before, so she hoped her sudden disappearance had succeeded in finally putting him off her tail. Peace of mind wouldn't come easy until she knew for sure though.

Speak of my phone. Lisa picked up her cell as it rang, noticing Jen's number. "Hi."

"Hey, just checking to make sure you're going tonight," Jen said.

"I planned on it, but after going through my things, I realized I didn't pack anything appropriate."

"No problem. Come on over, and if I don't have anything that fits you, we'll run into Boise. There's a little boutique that carries the best outfits for the club. I can tell Drew I'll meet him there, and we can go straight to Spurs after shopping."

Lisa had always shopped for club clothes online, and she'd never associated with other members in the lifestyle outside the private venues. The friends and co-workers she socialized with in Phoenix knew nothing about that part of her life. She'd liked taking in the dinner and movie with Kim and Debra from school last night but hoped neither woman learned of her extracurricular activities. She was still struggling to reconcile Jen's knowledge and similar interest.

After taking a mental calculation of her finances and remembering she got her first week's pay yesterday, she agreed to the impromptu plans. "I'd like that. Thanks, Jen."

"I should have thought of it sooner. Come over whenever you're ready. Bye."

Since this was likely her last night at Spurs, and with Shawn once she came clean with him, Lisa decided to go all out and get what relief she could before telling him who she was. It was too late to do much else, and bemoaning stupid mistakes and errors in judgment did no good. She wouldn't lie and say she didn't remember him or that night, but she also wouldn't humiliate herself more by telling him the reason she'd left Arizona. She didn't want to see the look on his face if he thought she'd run to him after all these years just so he could rescue her again.

With her cash all but depleted and blessed silence from her stalker for two weeks, she decided it was a good time to use her check to open a bank account and made the stop on her way to Jen's. Lisa couldn't remember the last time she'd purchased something new with pleasing a Dom in mind, but as she sifted through the lingerie and fetish clothes at the boutique with Jen, all she could think about was Shawn's reaction to seeing her in the revealing outfits.

"This would look great on you." Jen held up a demi bra and boy short set in lime-green satin, the bra cut low enough to show a hint of nipple, the shorts high enough to leave the undercurve of her butt cheeks bare.

"I like it." Taking the hanger, Lisa checked the price and winced. "Maybe not that much."

"Come on, splurge a little. Shawn won't be an easy man to hold onto for long. You may as well pull out all the stops while you can. I'll even cut your rent next month by the cost of the outfit."

Tickled, Lisa laughed and shook her head. "No, you won't. You already did me a huge favor by letting me sign a two-month lease instead of twelve. I'll get it and cut back on something else. I still have to cover the cost of an entry fee tonight."

Jen waved a hand and grabbed a black lace teddy and matching thong. "You know he'll waive it if you ask. He really is one of the good guys. Most of them are. Drew and I have known him, Clayton, and Dakota since high school, when they came to live with Buck Cooper."

"When we have more time, you'll have to tell me about him back then. I still haven't met the other two, only Master Simon," she said as they carried their selections to the counter.

"They were rebellious at first, got into a lot of trouble at school, but it didn't take Buck long to straighten them out. Between the three of them, I think they went through every girl in school," Jen replied, digging in her purse for her wallet while Lisa paid for hers.

Squashing an unexpected ripple of envy, Lisa smiled at Jen as she took the bag the clerk handed her. "Including you?"

"I wish sometimes, but no. Even back then, I only had eyes and hots for Drew. Speaking of which, we need to get going."

Her urgency rubbed off on Lisa, and she drove out to the club with anticipation humming through her veins, not to mention more than a small amount of anxiety over revealing her identity. The doors had just opened to members when they arrived and slipped into the restroom to change clothes.

"Go on in," Lisa told Jen as she left the enclosed commode and surveyed herself in the mirror. "I'll be right behind you."

"Catch you later. That looks great, by the way."

Sailing out with a breezy wave, she left Lisa alone with her worries and pondering how she would get through another scene while fretting about Shawn's reaction to her revelation.

****

"What's her name, the little girl we brought with us that night?"

Father Joe sighed as he walked through the quiet church, unsure how to answer Shawn's inquiry even though he'd known it would be coming ever since Lisa left town. "Hello to you, too," he returned dryly, leaving the sanctuary and following the connecting hall to his living quarters.

"Don't mess with me, Father. I need to know. It's important."

The boy's impatience came through the phone, alarming Joe. Even though he insisted, Shawn never dropped his respectful title unless he was angry or worried. "What's happened?" he asked with sharp concern, his gut tightening.

Shawn's short silence was followed by a change in his brusque tone to caution. "I've met someone new in town who seems familiar. Why would you think something untoward has occurred?"

Pushing his door closed, he leaned against it with a breath of relief. If this kept up, those two would put him in an early grave. "You said it was important, and, from your voice, I just assumed there was a problem."

"There is. I think I've met her before, and if I didn't know better, I'd swear she's the same kid I brought to you that night. But that's not possible, is it?"

"Anything is possible, son. You should know that."

"So, it is her. Lisa Halldor is her name, right?"

Joe wouldn't lie, not for either of them. "Yes, and yes I know she accepted a temporary job near you. I couldn't believe the coincidence, but all I told her was the three of you lived in the area. I never revealed your names as I hoped it would prevent an awkward reunion." All that was true, but he left it at that instead of telling him she insisted she didn't want to know anything else.

"So, it's a coincidence she's here, this close to me after all this time, huh? I was wondering if she even remembered that night, what happened after suffering such a shock."

Joe didn't like straddling this line between the two of them and wished Lisa had taken his advice and gone straight to Shawn with who she was and why she'd left town. It sounded like she'd gotten herself in a bind with her evasions and procrastinating, but he wouldn't interfere. The interest had been there all these years, for both of them. How they acted on it now was up to them.

"All I can tell you is she wanted to get away for a while and found that job. And, yes, I confirmed you lived there, leaving it up to her what she did knowing that. How much she remembers other than a teenage boy carrying her to safety, I don't know for sure as she doesn't talk about it. She's a nice girl, Shawn." *And as alone as you still are.* He knew better than to say that aloud.

"I never said she wasn't, except for her penchant to keep secrets."

Joe figured Lisa had her reasons, and he wouldn't butt in without her permission. He'd spoken with her a few days ago, relieved to hear she hadn't heard anything from her stalker since leaving. Maybe that was why she didn't feel the need to say anything to Shawn.

"I can't help you with any other questions about Lisa, Shawn."

"Can't, or won't, Father?"

Padding into the kitchen, he ended the conversation as abruptly as Shawn had started it. "I haven't eaten yet. Tell Clayton and Dakota hello. Goodbye, Shawn."

Shawn clicked off and shoved his cell in his back pocket, leaving the office at Spurs to join Clayton and Dakota at the bar as the doors opened. Father Joe's confirmation of Lisa's identity did little to appease him as he'd pretty much come to that conclusion on his own. There were several unanswered questions left, like why she hadn't told him who she was when she remembered him, leaving him no choice but to wait on her to answer them. He respected she might have her reasons, but if she showed up tonight, they couldn't continue in this vein, with secrets between them. Inside these walls, there was no room for secrets, something her experience would have taught her before she had come last week.

"Are you starting the night in a snit?" Clayton glanced at him with a raised brow as he brought his beer up for a long pull, leaning his other elbow on the bar top.

"Maybe. I haven't decided yet." Nodding his thanks to Ben who slid a beer over to him, Shawn remained standing, facing the bar, too edgy to sit.

Dakota's lips tilted at the corners, as close to a smile as he usually revealed. "That schoolteacher still getting under your skin a whole week later?"

"No, yes. Fuck. Shut up, both of you."

"No problem." Clayton stood and slapped him on the back. "I'd rather go play anyway."

"How about you?" Shawn asked Dakota. "We don't have to baby newbies tonight, so you're free, too." Dressed in his usual black, with his Stetson lowered and a forbidding set to his jaw, it was always a mystery to Shawn how Dakota could draw so much interest from women. But there was no denying he did, as several pairs of eyes were already aimed his way from submissive members sitting around the tables or on the sofas.

"I'm in no hurry."

Shawn chuckled. "You never are."

Shrugging his massive shoulders, Dakota turned toward the room, straightening as he appeared to spot someone who interested him. Shawn didn't think anything of it until his friend's slow drawl and next words held a wealth of meaning.

"You might want to get your shit together, fast."

Spinning around, his gaze zeroed in on Lisa walking toward him, her dainty breasts cupped by a neon-green half bra that revealed a peek of pink nipple. Matching shorts molded to her slim hips and emphasized her bare, slender legs. Even from a distance, there was no mistaking the need in her vivid eyes and etched on her pale face when she spotted him or the hint of uneasiness pinching her mouth.

She ought to worry about whatever game she had been playing with him since arriving in Mountain Bend. He did not like to lose.

"He's got it bad."

Shawn ignored Ben's comment to Dakota as he walked away from them to meet Lisa halfway. He did have it bad for her, but in what way, he still needed to figure out. It pissed him off she'd kept their prior association to herself these past two weeks, but he would remain open to hearing her explanation. Atkins' attempted molestation had to have been more traumatic for a young girl than the hits he'd subjected him, Clayton, and Dakota to suffer.

That didn't mean he wouldn't exact some form of retribution if she continued to deceive him though. Remembering what he'd walked in on that night, he would need to tread carefully so as not to trigger a painful memory without warning.

Fuck, why couldn't his first real interest in a woman be easy?

Lisa's eyes had widened when she'd seen him, the convulsive working of her slender throat to swallow another telltale sign of nerves. Shawn's pulse kicked up a notch as he considered those nerves, speculating whether they stemmed from a sub's natural reaction to putting herself in the hands of a Dom or from keeping a secret.

Without giving her time to think further, he held his hand out as soon as he reached her. "You're right on time. I like that, Lisa. Come sit with me."

"Okay."

She accepted his hand, her palm sweaty against his, her fingers trembling in his grip. Both jumpy signals were at odds with the glint of determination in her gaze and rigid set to her soft lips. He wasn't the only one sorting through questions about their association.

Spotting an empty table near the bar, he led her over and pulled her onto his lap as he took a seat. He flashed a wry grin at her look of consternation, releasing her hand to press against her hip as he moved his free hand to dip a finger under the edge of her bra and scoop out her nipple, baring it the rest of the way.

"Haven't any of your previous Doms placed you on

their lap?"

She shook her head, sending her blonde hair flying around her shoulders. "No. We always...I mean, I'm not much for socializing at these places."

Her nipple hardened under his circling finger, her eyes dilating with arousal as she squirmed on his thigh. "Sit still. We're not going to jump into a scene tonight. It's time I got to know more about you." She stiffened, and he pinched the tender bud. "Is that a problem?"

"It depends on what you want to know."

"Ah, honesty. Another point in your favor. Tell me, have you ever been dishonest with a Dom?" Keeping his eyes on her face, he continued to torment her nipple.

She bit her lip and struggled to swallow again even as she gave him a negative headshake. "No, I've only scened with three Masters before you, the last one I was with the longest and never told them, or you a lie."

"Good to know, but verbally telling a lie isn't the same as omission, is it?" he asked, shifting to free her other nipple and pluck it into a stiff peak.

Lisa paled then gasped with a shudder. He gave her a moment to form her thoughts, not surprised when he caught a quick flash of annoyance cross her face before she pasted on a blank expression.

"I'm not sure what you're getting at, Sir, but I don't see the need to reveal a lot about myself when I won't be here long. Maybe you should pick someone else for tonight."

Shawn tightened his hold on her hip as she made to get up, leaving his nipple play to press against her abdomen. "I don't want someone else tonight." He hardened his voice as he added, "If you do, say red, and we're done, not just tonight though, but for good."

As he thought, she didn't like that idea any more than he. She was as attuned to him as he was to her, their connection undeniable whether she chose to accept that or not. Clayton took that moment to saunter over, a wicked grin curling his mouth as he pulled out a chair, turned it, and straddled the seat. As usual, his timing sucked.

Shawn frowned at him. "What happened to *your* girl? Did she turn you down?"

Clayton's grin widened. "Nope, she's in the restroom, so I have a minute. It's nice to see you again, Lisa." He thumbed back his tan Stetson, revealing the curious glint in his blue eyes before his gaze slid to caress Lisa's pretty reddened nipples.

"You've met?"

"Master Simon introduced us." Lisa smiled at Clayton. "Thank you, Sir. Nice to see you again also."

She rested her hands on his arm at her waist, and Shawn took note of the absence of unease with Clayton's arrival, admiring her obvious pleasure in a stranger's blatant attention to her exposed nipples. He'd noticed last week how comfortable she appeared with public nudity and was interested in learning if that resulted from her time as a submissive or if exhibition aroused her.

"You're the new teacher. Where was your mother when I was in school?" Clayton teased. "I wouldn't have minded going to class near as much if I had a pretty face like yours to look at."

That innocent question elicited her first reaction to Clayton, a jump in her pulse against his arm, and when Shawn glanced at her face, he saw the smile she gave Clayton slip.

Before he could intervene, she replied, "She's been gone a long time. You would have been a teenager."

"I'm sorry, darlin'." Clayton cut him a quizzical look, as if he now found something familiar about Lisa.

Shawn shouldn't care if putting her on the spot made her uncomfortable, but he did, and sought to intervene before his friend said anything else. "Go away, Clayton."

"Got it." With a gleam in his eyes, he stood and leaned over to lift Lisa's face with two fingers under her chin. He planted a quick, hard kiss on her mouth then said, "When you've had enough of this guy, come find me." With a wink, he spun on his booted heel and went to the bar.

"Huh." Lisa brushed her lower lip with two fingers, her look bemused as she watched Clayton walk away.

The painful stab of jealousy in Shawn's gut was new, and he didn't know what to make of it. Tabling that questionable reaction for later, he picked up where they'd left off, hoping to entice her into staying instead of backing away. Her spandex shorts dipped low on her waist and cut high on her legs, making it easy for him to slip his fingers inside the stretchy material.

"What will it be, Lisa? Continue?" The shorts lowered with his hand until he came into contact with the soft, bare skin of her damp labia. "Or stop?"

As if that was no choice at all, she lifted into his

hand on a quiet moan. "Continue, please, Sir."

"Excellent. Where were we?" Inching lower, he slid his middle finger between her plump folds to trace along the slick seam. "I remember, getting to know you better. Where in Arizona did you live?"

"Doesn't most of the population reside in the Phoenix area?"

Displeased, he pinched the tender flesh of one delicate fold. "That's not an answer."

"It's hard to think," she snapped back then bit her lip as she likely realized that wasn't a wise tone to take.

"And yet, you managed another evasive answer that was no answer." His eyes bored into hers as he speared her pussy with a deep-fingered thrust. "Want to try again?"

Lisa blew out a frustrated breath with a jerky nod, her chest lifting with a deep inhale. "All I remember before losing my mother was our small apartment and the elderly neighbor who came over when Mom went to work on the night shift. And, yes, we lived in the Phoenix area, where, I couldn't say." She paused to gasp as he added a finger and scissored inside her tight depth. "Other than that, I don't recall. Sir, *please.*" Her hips lifted again, this time her thighs falling open wider.

Her strangled plea got to him on a level no previous encounter had managed. Unable to resist, he swirled his fingers in her silken pussy, enjoying the tight squeeze of her vaginal walls even as he contemplated how much time had lapsed since she'd last indulged in sex. Some subs wouldn't go that far at a club; others embraced everything. Shawn circled her swollen clit then rubbed the sensitive tissue between his fingers. "Concentrate on your body, and what I'm doing, nothing else, and, this time, give me a better orgasm than last week," he insisted, pressing harder on her clit.

Holding her close, he manipulated her clit and bent his head to take one straining nipple into his mouth, both nubbins hardening under his fingers and tongue. Lisa dug her nails into his arm, her breathing turning ragged as she arched into his marauding hand. Alternating between strong pulls on both tender buds and softer caresses, he brought her to a feverish pitch in moments.

But he wanted more.

Releasing her clit and nipple, he delivered three deep, rapid thrusts inside her soaked pussy and sank his teeth into her neck. Her startled inhale followed with a whimper as she quivered against him, and he relished the spurt of cream coating his fingers. "Now, Lisa," he ordered, returning to her clit and nipple with voracious force.

Shawn wanted to smile as she splintered apart, gushing over his fingers and hand, her inner muscles clamping around them with spasmodic clutches.

That's more like it.

****

Lisa writhed and basked in the glory of a mind-numbing orgasm as Master Shawn kept her pinned against the thick muscles of his wide chest and shoulder. His quads and arm muscles bunched under her thighs and hands, his strength a calming antidote to the storm of pleasure drenching her senses. On some level, she'd always maintained an awareness of her surroundings when with a Dom, but not this time, not with this man.

The place and people were lost in her subconscious, shoved aside to make room for the brief freedom of an out-of-body, euphoric experience. Attaining a measure of relief from the stress of keeping quiet about their past, Shawn's constant poking about his suspicions, and the weeks of torment by her stalker was a heady trip she didn't want to return from. Unfortunately, her body gave her no choice as she slowly drifted down from the shattering high, the lyrics of another country western tune infiltrating her fogged head, along with the low murmur of voices. A woman's high-pitched cry brought her eyes open as Lisa realized Shawn's hand was still between her legs, his fingers lightly caressing her throbbing flesh. No wonder leftover climatic ripples continued to course through her body.

She registered his comforting embrace next and wished his arms didn't feel so good wrapped around her, that she didn't relish having someone to lean on so much.

Unable to look at him yet, knowing what she would have to say next, she glanced toward the wall, surprised to see Master Simon wielding a wicked looking cane across the red-striped buttocks of a woman bound facing the St. Andrew's Cross. His dark face revealed a sternness he'd reined in around her, as did the next forceful swing of the thin rod. The woman showed her willingness for his harsh strokes by pushing her butt out to receive the blow.

Lisa shuddered then sucked in a fortifying breath and forced herself to say, "We have met before, a long time ago, only I didn't know who you were until you stopped to change my flat." She swiveled her head upward, blowing out a breath when she saw his face. "And you've already figured out when and where."

Shawn nodded. "Father Joe confirmed my suspicions. The question remains, why didn't you?"

Because I recognized you right away, and it hurt when you didn't remember me. None of that was supposed to happen. Lisa wasn't about to admit that embarrassing tidbit. "It's been such a long time, we were so young, and it was only what, two or three hours before Father called the authorities and we were separated? I barely remember going to him, and when you didn't recognize me, I let it go."

Dragging his hand out of her lowered shorts, he left a damp trail on her abdomen and each nipple with a light brush of his fingers before reaching her neck and pressing his palm against her throat. She shuddered at the slight compression and power move that accompanied the darkening of his silver gaze to pewter.

"But once we hooked up here, our relationship went from casual acquaintances to Dom/sub, and you knew better than to answer a direct question with anything less than the full truth, did you not?"

Oh boy, am I in trouble. Lisa nodded, running through possible punishments he might mete out, growing warm at the possibilities popping up in her head. "Yes, I'm sorry. I didn't know how you would react, and didn't want to risk..." *A return of the coldness.* "You were on the verge of breaking through a mental block that's plagued me for a while."

He pressed his fingers into the side of her neck before letting go and dropping his hand to her lowered waistband again. "Understandable but still punishable."

A shiver skated down her spine even before she realized his intent and he flipped her onto her stomach, across his knees. Shoving her shorts down, he exposed her bare butt to the cooler air and everyone mingling nearby. Lisa jumped with a gasped, "Oh!" as he tapped her right cheek then laid his hand over the tingling spot.

"Have you ever earned a punishment from a Dom before?" he asked with a casual caress over both buttocks.

Lisa huffed a laugh, grabbing his calf to keep her balance. "No, and I've never been spanked by anyone. Hard to believe, huh?"

"It tells me your previous Doms were neglectful in your education. You don't have to disobey a rule to earn a new lesson. I'll give you credit for thinking you had a good reason for evading the truth with me after I correct your assumption. The safeword applies in this scenario as well."

Master Shawn gave her no time to contemplate what he meant by "credit" as he robbed her of air with the first hard swat. Prickly heat and sharp pain blossomed across her buttock, and she clenched against the sting seeping into her flesh. The next smack was just as hard, covering her opposite buttock, the burn and pain mirroring its twin. For the first time since entering a private club, she debated whether to continue or bail out.

The third blow landed in the center of both cheeks, striking with enough force to shake her butt and bring a watery sheen to her eyes. With just three spanks, he'd left her aching and throbbing, the heat sinking deep into her quivering muscles. He rubbed the offended areas, the slight scratchiness of his calloused palm drawing a shudder, and Lisa welcomed the softer touch with a sigh.

"Oh God," she moaned, jerking from the sudden lightning bolt of pleasure striking her lower half as he slid a finger up between her buttocks and glided over the sensitive pucker of her anus. Struggling to maintain her equilibrium as he resumed his soothing touch, she braved a look up at him, her throat going dry at the carnal set to his mouth and the appreciative glint in his eyes. The lingering soreness from those hard spanks eased into a distracting twinge, the pulsating warmth spreading to her empty pussy and producing a surprising return of dampness.

"Sir, are you done?" That wasn't disappointment lacing her tone, was it? She didn't want more of those blistering smacks but had to admit she enjoyed his callous-abrasive exploration of her backside.

The corners of that sexy-as-sin mouth curved upward, her toes curling in response. "With phase one, yes. Phase two is just as much fun. You have a world-class ass, Lisa."

A warm fuzzy encompassed her chest every time he said her name with that drawling inflection in his voice. "Thanks." She put her head back down, the tenseness slipping from her body with each caress, squeeze, and scrape of his nails across her sensitive skin.

Lisa had never been so aware of her backside, the round, fleshy cheeks made for one purpose – to sit on – in her mind. But under Master Shawn's tutelage, she was learning differently. Every light stroke over her skin and deep-fingered compression into her fleshy globes drew a tremble for more. Her empty sheath dampened and spasmed for attention, and even though he stayed away from making a return, she was content lying there, letting him continue playing.

Until he started a rhythmic, light spanking across both cheeks, just enough to stir the warmth back to the forefront and remind her of the ache. She shifted in growing arousal as she found herself enjoying those softer smacks, the tingles they elicited spreading down her legs and up to her nipples. A titillating shiver danced down her spine as she eyed the large boots and smaller bare feet walking by them.

With a pat on the undercurve of one buttock, he left her backside humming in pleasure to grip her hair and tug her head up. "You're not falling asleep on me, are you?"

Almost. "No." With a rare blush of embarrassment staining her face, she accepted his help sitting up, grateful for his support as he stood her between his spread thighs and she wobbled.

Shawn pulled up her shorts, saying, "Now you can say you've experienced spanking." He tugged up her bra cups and stood, clasping her hand. "Come with me, and I'll get you some water. We need to talk more but maybe not tonight. You look like you could use time to figure out where you want to go with me from here, and so do I about you."

"Yes, that's a good idea."

But as she drove home thirty minutes later, Lisa realized how limited her options were since her life was still waiting for her return to Phoenix.

CHAPTER SIX

66You're not working on your campaign."

Shawn didn't bother to hide his annoyance with Lyle. He'd had a few things on his mind since throwing his hat in the ring for sheriff, like one attractive blonde who continued to tug on his conscience. He understood meeting him on the county road her first day here had thrown her for a loop when she somehow recognized him after all these years. He also understood and appreciated her reserve in admitting their previous connection, considering the long passage of time.

But, in the past two weeks, she had ample time and opportunities to learn more about him and come clean with the truth. Then there were the unanswered questions still running through his head to deal with, like why had she taken a temporary position so far from home, and what, or who was responsible for the glimpses of fear and worry he'd caught on her expressive face and lurking in her eyes a few times?

Shutting down his computer, he stood, noticing Kevin had already checked out for the day. "I'm bogged down with other responsibilities," he told Lyle, reaching for his Stetson on the desk and slapping it on his head. "If I get caught up soon, I'll get on it. If not, I'll drop out."

Lyle frowned, indicating his displeasure. "I wish you wouldn't."

"What do you have against the other two

candidates? Both are seasoned deputies with good records."

"They aren't from this county though. Sandusky's from Boise, in Ada County. He's a hard ass, used to dealing with the crime that comes with a larger population and unfamiliar with our rural ways."

Shawn shook his head, believing they should give the guy a chance if the voters chose him. "We're only thirty miles from the county line, and Boise, and we've had our share of crime."

Lyle remained stubborn. "Our entire county has a fraction of the population of the capital alone. And I flat-out don't like Roberts. People won't forget he resigned from our department to take that cushy job in Montana only to return here a year later with no explanation for his change of mind."

Shawn agreed with him about Roberts. The guy was a weasel. "I'll give it my best shot, that's all I can promise. I'm off until Sunday, so see you Monday. In the meantime, *you* might consider staying on for one more term." Which would work for Shawn and the community. Despite his stubbornness, Lyle was a good man.

His thoughts jumped right back to Lisa as he slid behind the wheel of his cruiser. He sat a moment, running through options for gaining her trust even as he asked himself why he was bothering, given her short residency in Mountain Bend. There was no denying he liked her. Between admiring her gumption in packing up and leaving the only place she'd ever lived to take a short-term job and enjoying the contrast between her submissive sexual nature and those sparks of annoyed defiance he'd caught in her eyes, he found it difficult to keep his distance.

She intrigued him, and given he had experienced that same tug of protectiveness he'd felt all those years ago more than once since they'd reunited, he wasn't about to walk away yet. There must be a reason she had chosen to come here knowing the three of them lived in Mountain Bend. And a reason she'd left Arizona in the first place. Those unanswered questions, coupled with his dominant physical attraction, made her impossible to resist.

Starting the engine, Shawn decided he'd given her enough time to gather her thoughts and to recoup from their scene and discussion last weekend. Since it was after five, he swung through Charlie's Chicken and picked up dinner then drove to the bungalow she rented from the Zimmermans, hoping to catch her at home. Turning the corner onto Maple, he spotted her yellow VW first then saw her pushing a lawn mower along the side of the duplex.

With her head down and a fierce expression of determination on her face, Lisa didn't notice as he parked behind her car, got out, and leaned against his cruiser with his arms crossed. Her slim arms strained as she struggled to get through the overgrown grass, and, from the odd pattern and missed areas in the mowed front, it appeared she was new to yard work. She looked up at the same time as she pulled back with the mower then quickly jumped to avoid running over her foot. The scowl she sent him as she cut the engine off indicated she blamed him.

"What are you doing here?" Lisa huffed, looking none too pleased as she walked toward him, brushing her hair off her perspiring face with the back of her hand.

Considering the late afternoon cooler temperature, he figured her strain with getting the job done accounted for her overheated appearance. Reaching into the open window, he held up the food bag. "I took a chance you haven't eaten yet and got you a chicken platter, along with me. Take this." She grabbed the bag, and he retrieved two drinks from the cupholder. "Coke for you, right?" His timing was perfect. She eyed the Coke with thirst.

"Yes, and not that I'm ungrateful, but you could have checked with me first." She snatched the Coke, handing him back the dinner, and took a long drink through the straw. "*Ahhh*, that tasted good." She blinked, as if coming out of a sugar-induced trance, and her eyes turned wary. "What do you really want, Shawn?"

"A simple dinner and conversation. Come on, let's eat while it's hot, and then I'll show you what you're doing wrong out here."

Lisa glanced around the small yard, her face falling as she took in the clumps of tall grass where she'd missed running the mower. "I guess I didn't do such a good job, huh? I've only lived in apartments, but I was hoping to repay the Zimmermans for the short lease agreement by saving them some time on this chore."

"It's not that bad. Lead the way inside. It'll still be light enough to finish up out here after we eat."

She let out a sigh, shoulders slumping as she pivoted. "Okay, but only because that smells too good to turn down."

"Of course."

Shawn eyed the enticing fit of her jeans over her ass as he followed her into the kitchen, remembering the softness of her pliable cheeks and the way her pale skin reddened so nicely. He'd stopped at three punishing swats since it was her first time over a Dom's knee, but he'd made sure they were hard enough for the discomfort to linger for a while. Playing with her delectable butt had been as much fun as spanking the heart-shaped globes.

"Have you picked up Charlie's since coming here?" he asked, handing her the covered platter before taking the seat across from her at the small table.

"No. I've only gone to the B&B's buffet and to the restaurant with you." She scooped up a forkful of creamy mashed potatoes and hummed in appreciation, the low murmur going straight to Shawn's cock. "These are good," she said, taking another heaping bite.

"Try the chicken. It's even better. Will you join me at Spurs tomorrow night?"

Her hand paused on the way to her mouth, a closed expression replacing the pleasure she'd shown in the food. Maybe giving her time to settle her thoughts this week was the wrong thing to do as it gave her time to erect the shields he'd noticed right off.

"I don't think so. Given my temporary stay, it's probably not a good idea to get involved any deeper."

"We're already involved, so that's a moot point. If that's your way of saying sex is off the table, I can respect that." He might not like it, but it wasn't the first time a woman passed on taking things that far. Instead of pushing her, he went in a different direction. "But, that's fine. If you haven't visited a working ranch before, that's something you don't want to miss out on before returning to Phoenix. Spend Saturday with me at our place. I'll take you riding, and we can fish for trout to grill."

Shawn smiled, seeing the quick flare of longing and excitement on her face before she masked it and shifted her focus out the window. He wasn't above playing dirty to persuade her. Reaching across the table, he gripped her chin, and her gaze swung back to him. "You want to, so admit it and say yes. I'd like to hear about the family Father Joe found for you to live with after I carried you away from Atkins, and what made you go into teaching and prompted you to take the short-term job here." Dropping his hand, he buttered a biscuit, adding, "I asked Father about you several times during those first months, but he refused to say anything other than you were adjusting. You've kept in touch with him, so you know how close-mouthed he can get."

"You asked about me? I thought...never mind."

The surprise in her voice cut him to the quick. All these years, he'd thought she wouldn't remember much about that night, including him, not enough to feel hurt believing he'd forgotten all about her. "I wouldn't risk a kidnapping rap just to walk away without making sure you were better off. That just goes to show how little we know about each other. This time around, I would like to rectify that, wouldn't you?"

Lisa busied herself cutting a piece of chicken breast, spearing it with her fork and waiting until she swallowed to answer, the wheels of serious contemplation going on in her head reflected on her face. He ran through his options if she refused then she finally replied, and he was able to put away the drastic measures he was considering.

"Thanks for the offer. I'd like to see your ranch. I've never ridden, and it sounds like fun."

Shawn noticed she didn't shy away from getting on a horse, and she didn't admit she wanted to get to know more about him, but he suspected she was as curious as he. It was a start, something to build on before he could delve into what had brought her here and what caused the block she mentioned overcoming at the club.

****

Phoenix

"Gotcha," Bruce crowed as he hung up from the sleazeball investigator he'd finally broken down and taken the risk of hiring to unearth Lisa Halldor's whereabouts.

It had taken some doing, first finding someone disreputable enough to break a few laws getting into private records then offering enough monetary enticement to get the job done quickly without getting caught. For two weeks, he'd waited to hear back from him, all the while forced to listen to the old man's complaints about his failure to bring him the daughter he'd ignored for most of her life.

Near death experiences apparently had a way of changing a person, his father being a prime example. No matter, Bruce thought, stalking out of the office to pour himself a drink. He would personally ensure the two never met and be there for the old man to comfort him through his grief after learning of her unfortunate demise.

Carrying his whiskey out to the veranda, he settled in his favorite chair and took in the Arizona sunset across the vast, untouched desert landscape. He wasn't about to lose half his inheritance, which would cost him an unacceptable portion of his current lifestyle, including this property in the elite, gated community he couldn't afford without his dad's money. With its privacy, killer views, and top-of-the-line amenities, he couldn't imagine living anywhere else after enjoying these luxuries for so long. Then there were his creditors breathing down his neck to add to his reasons for making sure he was the only one to reap the benefits of his father's labors.

If a young woman had to lose her life for him to keep what was rightfully his in the first place, so be it. His father had raised him to be a ruthless businessman; it wasn't his fault the callous heartlessness Frank had instilled in him extended to beyond business dealings.

Bruce waited until he reached Idaho and got settled into a motel outside of Boise, about twenty-five miles from Mountain Bend where Halldor purportedly resided, to make his plans. He'd told his father he was leaving on a short business trip, but that he had people still looking for his daughter. Frank hadn't been happy, but then, that was nothing new. He'd been impossible to live with, a changed man since recovering from his massive heart attack. Halldor's sudden disappearance hadn't improved Frank's, or Bruce's disposition for that matter, and he decided she needed to pay for the extra grief she'd caused him.

He would let her live a little longer for the payback fun of watching her squirm in fear. As he unpacked and climbed into the lumpy, uncomfortable bed and listened to the traffic outside the window, he added the necessity of staying in such a place to his list of grievances against her.

****

Temporary, lust-induced insanity. That's the only excuse I can come up with. Lisa gripped the steering wheel as she turned off the main road and drove between the brick entrance posts to Shawn's property Saturday morning, asking herself what the heck had gotten into her. She didn't need the angst of spending more time with the man she kept obsessing over. Hadn't tormenting herself last night by imagining Master Shawn at his club with another willing submissive been enough self-abuse and misery to put herself through? She'd enjoyed his surprise visit the other night way too much for her peace of mind. Add in the prickling jealousy still cramping her abdomen and her hopes of returning home unscathed from meeting her one-time protector were shot to hell.

"A bad case of the hots and curiosity, that's all that's going on," she muttered as she drank in the picturesque vista spread out before her.

Ranging cattle herds dotted the vast acreage of

wild prairie land, and, if she wasn't mistaken, a few shaggy-haired, lumbering bison. A shimmering small lake offered water, with the ponderosa and lodgepole pines providing ample shade. She could catch the scent of pine on the light breeze coming in her rolled down window as she took in the snow-capped mountains looming skyward in the background.

Following Shawn's instructions, she veered left and took the smooth dirt road to the log house he had described. Parking in the circle drive, she got out and admired the well-kept lawn and shrubs. From the pointers he'd given her on mowing, she suspected he took care of his own grass despite his busy schedule. How he kept up with his jobs as a deputy sheriff, part owner of this ranch, and now invested in a private club, she couldn't begin to guess.

Lisa stood outside enjoying the sun on her face and the faint lowing of cattle reaching her ears, pondering how long she could procrastinate before letting Shawn know she was here, and how she could keep herself from wanting more from him than a day spent as casual acquaintances. Then he stepped out onto the front porch, and her heart executed a slow roll again, that funny feeling that hinted it wasn't just her body craving more from the deputy sheriff slash rancher.

Screw it, she thought, eyeing his tall frame, broad shoulders, and rugged face, a curl of arousal settling low in her abdomen. She wanted this day with him, a few hours free of worrying about a crazy person stalking her, to enjoy his company without the secret of their first encounter standing between them.

Shawn came down the steps, his loose-limbed stride revealing the strength of his quad muscles contracting under the tight denim, the black belt cinched around his slim hips conjuring up new fantasies she'd never contemplated before. Looking up at his chiseled, tanned face, beard-shadowed jaw, and into the suggestive purpose in his potent, gunmetal gaze nearly stripped away the last of her defenses.

"Have any trouble finding your way here?" he asked, grasping her hand.

Lisa wished she didn't like that sign of possessiveness or the tight clasp of his much larger hand engulfing her smaller one so much. "No, your instructions were good. Oh!" She stumbled to a stop behind him as two German shepherds came bounding toward them from the back of the cabin.

"Mo, Curly, back." Shawn held his free hand palm out toward the dogs and they halted a foot from them, looking at him with adoration in their dark eyes and tongues lolling out. "Good boys," he crooned in a tone she'd never heard him use.

She grinned as he scratched behind their ears, one at a time, the dogs' obvious trust easing the tension their sudden appearance had produced. Having never owned a pet, she'd never understood the bond between a dog and owner, but there was no denying Shawn's attachment to the pair.

Tugging her up next to him, he gave her a reassuring glance. "They're friendly if you want to pet them. I adopted them from a rescue shelter not long ago, and they've come a long way with a healthy, steady diet and socialization. But even so, they've never shown a sign of aggression, which is surprising, given the breed and their previous neglect."

Twenty years and he is still saving kids, and now animals, she mused, recalling the article on Shawn's rescue of the young boy who had fallen down a well. She needed to remember part of his interest in her stemmed from his nature to jump in and help those in jeopardy, the other part as a Dom intent on fixing whatever had been holding her back.

Reaching a tentative hand toward the closest dog, Lisa sank her fingers into his thick fur and got a lick on her wrist that tickled. "He's soft." She frowned, feeling his ribs. "And still too skinny."

"Yeah, that'll take time. Once they've put on more weight and can handle the extra exercise, I'll take them on the range with me. But right now, I have to put them in the house before we leave. I just installed a dog door and built a fenced run on the other side so they're not cooped up all day." He nodded toward an oversized truck parked next to his department-issued cruiser. "Let me help you into the cab then give me a minute to take them inside."

"Where will we be going?" she asked, patting the other dog before following Shawn, smiling when the pair trotted behind them.

"To the stables, where Dakota has a docile mare picked out for you. You can get used to her in the corral first then I'll take you on a trail ride to the creek that has the best fishing." He opened the passenger door, releasing her hand to lift her onto the seat.

Grasping his shoulders for balance, Lisa found

herself at eye level with him, their faces a mere inch apart, his eyes going dark and her pulse skipping a beat. She moistened her suddenly dry lips, wanting him to close the small gap between their mouths in the worst way.

His hands tightened on her waist as he growled, "Fuck," and took possession of her mouth.

Digging her nails into his thick muscles, she groaned at the insistence of his tongue stroking hers, sweeping her gums, then returning to taste her again. His lips moved with hard aggression over hers, working her mouth until she couldn't tell them apart. The ball of heat his touch produced in her stomach slowly unfurled to spread up to her breasts and down to her pussy. His hands slid from her waist to her butt, pushing her forward on the seat as he spread her knees with his. She grew hot with arousal, quivering as he settled between them, pressing his denim-encased, thick erection against her mound while easing up on her mouth just enough to sink his teeth into the soft flesh of her lower lip.

"Shawn, this..."

He stroked his tongue over the sting, soothing the throb that matched the ache between her legs. "Not a good idea, I know," he finished for her before pulling away and dropping his hands. "I'll be right back."

Lisa touched her lip, watching him interact with the dogs on the way to the house, her heart heavy. No good could come of letting him touch her again, but she seemed unable to resist. The heartbreak she was courting just might be worth it to pass the next few weeks submitting to his possession.

The drive to the stables took about ten minutes,

and on the way, Shawn told her a little about the Coopers, who had taken the three of them in, and Buck's recent death.

"You really cared for him." It was there in his voice and the sadness in his eyes.

"Yeah, we all did. Shocked the hell out of us when he left us in charge of this spread. Miss Betty was happy to move to Mountain Bend, and into the one retirement neighborhood where she had friends who were also widows." He pointed to the forested area on the right. "Buck caught us hanging out in there instead of going to school one morning. How the hell he knew we skipped is still unknown, but we paid the price when he made us spend the day polishing every saddle and oiling all the tack then writing apologies to each teacher. He never raised his voice, didn't have to. He could come across as disappointed and pissed at the same time."

"And you stayed."

He nodded. "We stayed. Despite the hard work and the rules we weren't used to, the three of us admitted to each other we were intrigued by the change from everything we'd grown up with. The education in caring for livestock and farming crops was a lot more interesting than algebra and English lit."

"I liked school," she admitted but could see how this ranch with its endless open ranges, woods, and creeks that offered the chance for teenage boys to ride and work in the outdoors could alter their adolescent bad behavior.

Shawn flipped her a rueful grin as he parked in front of a massive stable painted beige with red trim and surrounded by several other, equally large, similar buildings. "You were a shy book geek, weren't you?"

Returning his smile, she opened her door. "Yes, but I don't regret skipping the wild parties I was never invited to anyway. My studying got me a scholarship, which I needed since my foster family's obligation ended when I turned eighteen." A look of compassion crossed his face, and to defuse the awkward moment, she nodded toward the tall man with American Indian features standing by a corral. "Is that Dakota? I think I saw him at Spurs."

"That's him. Don't let his size and scowl bother you. He doesn't like to let people know he's really a pussycat," he replied with an undertone of amusement as he alit from the truck.

Lisa was more interested in the brown-and-white dappled mare tethered to the fence rail, her large doe eyes reflecting a sweet disposition. Shawn snatched her hand again, his touch a quick reminder of the heat his kiss had generated.

It was going to be a long day.

"Dakota, this is Lisa. Angel is a good pick for her. Thanks."

Craning her neck to look up at the man whose face was sun-kissed darker than Shawn's, she guessed his intimidating height reached at least six foot four. "It's nice to meet you," she said when he didn't respond.

"Welcome to the Rolling Hills Ranch. Like Shawn said, Angel here won't give you any trouble." He turned his midnight eyes toward Shawn. "I need to go over a few things with you."

"No problem." Shawn flagged down a young

cowhand working just inside the open stable doors before telling Lisa, "I'll help you mount, and Scotty will lead you around for a few minutes."

Lisa nodded, smiling at the hired hand as Shawn introduced them and asked for his assistance.

"Glad to," Scotty replied, tipping his hat to her. "Miss."

"They're bigger up close." She caressed the silky nose as Angel leaned her head over the rail, unable to resist the mare's friendly nudge against her shoulder.

Shawn took her elbow. "And she's one of our smaller horses. Come inside so I can boost you up. Scotty, walk her around and stay close. This is her first time."

"Yes, sir. I won't let you fall, miss."

He was so polite and earnest, Lisa couldn't help but like him. "I'm not worried, Scotty."

At least, not about getting on the horse. She was concerned about her growing need for Shawn as he led her into the corral and stood behind her to place her hands on the saddle pommel then press his big body against her back. His warm breath tickled her neck as he leaned close to say, "Put your foot in the stirrup and I'll give you a boost."

His warm breath tickled her neck as he leaned close to say, "Put your foot in the stirrup and I'll give you a boost."

Since her brain didn't seem to be functioning on all cylinders and his nearness snagged her breath, Lisa didn't try modifying her voice to sound unaffected. "Okay." Her breath released on a gasp as he lifted her at the waist and she swung her leg over the saddle, the sudden height offering an expanded view across the pastureland for as far as she could see.

"Oh, it's breathtaking," she said in awe.

"Wait until we start riding. I'll be right back. Hold on tight," he replied, handing Scotty the reins.

Lisa's focus switched from Shawn to enjoying the slow rocking atop the mare as Scotty strolled around the corral, leading the mare. Loving everything about the new venture, she soon found her rhythm and grew at ease riding the gentle horse. Scotty gave her pointers and a mini-lesson on how to steer, start, and stop, and by the time Shawn returned, she was more than ready to leave the enclosure and try a faster gait.

****

Shawn's plans for the afternoon hadn't included kissing Lisa so soon after she arrived or pushing her buttons by keeping close and constantly touching her. But she was too damn irresistible, especially when she didn't think he noticed the flashes of lust crossing her face or the vulnerable need reflected in her eyes. He imagined sexual attraction was as easy for her to identify and admit to as it was for him, yet she seemed less inclined to embrace exploring the deeper relationship he found himself leaning toward.

The key to opening her mind to that possibility lay in finding out what had driven her here in the first place, and why she didn't want him to know. While he did enjoy a puzzle and a challenge, he was conscious of his growing desire to have her stay in

Mountain Bend and how little time he had to make that happen.

As she rode alongside him across the prairies, he admired the ease with which she'd taken to riding. The smile that had kicked up as they'd ridden out of the corral and hadn't slipped in the last thirty minutes revealed her pleasure, the sidelong glances she likely thought he was blind to conveyed interest in more than riding. He liked seeing her so relaxed, having fun, her eyes clear of troubling shadows.

"Tug your reins to the left," he instructed as they neared a trail bisecting the wooded area up ahead. "We'll take that path through the trees to the creek."

Looking toward the path, her brows furrowed. "It looks narrow."

"Stay behind me. You'll be fine. Angel knows the way, so all you have to do is sit tight."

Her doubt cleared, and she flashed him a broad grin. "I've got that part down pat."

"Yes, you do," he murmured, thinking that could also apply to her reservations about getting involved with him.

Shawn never tired of the fresh, combined scents of pines, firs, and red cedar that assailed his nostrils as soon as he entered the woods. The constant racket of busy squirrels hopping from tree to tree and the flutter of twittering birds made up for the lack of conversation until they came out at the wide, fast-flowing creek.

"What do you think?" he asked her, dismounting then reaching up to help her down.

"It's beautiful. Is there anything besides trout?"

"Not a fan, huh?" he replied when she wrinkled her

nose. "Some steelhead, Mountain Whitefish, bass, a few more. It's a little early, but the salmon is great."

"I love salmon but never knew you could find it in rivers."

"We'll come out again in a few weeks." Holding her close, he felt a small shudder go through her. Pleased with that response, he tugged the fishing poles out of his saddle, saying, "The Salmon River feeds into several creeks. We're lucky enough to have one of them running through our property. Grab that blanket tucked into your saddlebag, will you?"

"Sure."

Another satisfied kick struck him with her reluctance to disengage from his light hold. Stepping back, he waited until she turned toward Angel then swatted her ass before hiking down to a grassy spot on the bank. The start of April had bumped the temperature into the upper fifties, and with the sun shining high, they would have a pleasant afternoon. He should feel guilty for bailing on his ranch responsibilities for a few hours, but he could make it up to Clayton and Dakota later. If he only had a limited time with the girl he'd never forgotten in all these years, he wanted to take advantage of every moment.

"Just so you know," Lisa said as she reached him with the blanket over her arm, "I'm as ignorant about fishing as riding."

"There's not much to it. Bait the line, toss it in, and wait for a nibble."

Shawn smiled when she wrinkled her nose as he slid a worm onto each hook. Setting his rod down, he moved behind her and placed the smaller one in her hands, showing her how to hold it.

"Okay, now bring your arm back over your shoulder and fling the line as far out as you can." Her head came up to his chest, her soft butt a nice cushion for his hips as he guided her swing. "Excellent. You're in a good spot." Taking his hands off hers, he heard her breathing hitch as he slid them up her arms then down her sides, brushing the plump curves of her breasts before settling at her waist. "Get comfortable on the blanket while I throw my line."

Turning her face toward his, she licked her lips, her eyes conveying his success in heightening her senses. "What are you fishing for, Shawn, other than trout?"

"I did mention last weekend we should get to know each other better. You can start by telling me more about your life in Phoenix." He turned to pick up his rod and flick the line into the creek, his aim perfect as it sank into the water several feet from hers. "Come on, sit down."

Lisa gave in to the inevitable and sat next to him, forcing herself to ignore the low, simmering arousal his light touches and constant nearness had produced. She didn't mind telling him about herself, maybe because she'd enjoyed hearing the respect and caring in his voice when he'd spoken of the couple who'd taken the three teenagers in, and his adjustment to living here, so far from home. But she knew it was wise to keep reminding herself his interest meant no more than a Dom's obligation toward a sub, or an old acquaintance wanting to appease his curiosity about a young girl he'd stepped in to help a long time ago.

She'd decided to take what she could get while she could and stifled the growing ache for more as she told him about her college days and landing her dream job of teaching first grade at a small, private elementary school right after graduation.

"You don't mention dating or affairs," he said when she paused.

She stifled her pique with a shrug. "I didn't think you'd be interested, besides, there isn't much to tell. I went out very little during college, and when I did, it never amounted to more than a movie or dinner. I dated a fellow teacher at the parochial school for a year, but when we split, things turned awkward, and I ended up changing jobs. After that disappointment, I made sure I didn't go out with a colleague again."

Shawn rested his rod on his bent leg and leaned back on one arm, his Stetson tugged low enough to hide his eyes, so she couldn't tell what he thought of that personal disclosure. His mouth tightened then curled in that way that pumped her blood flowing faster.

"He sounds like a wimp. Who came after him?"

Frowning, she switched her gaze back to watching her line for a tug. "Why? Are you going to tell me about every woman you've slept with?"

"Nope, because there's been no one who has left a lasting impression. From the hurt in your tone, the breakup with that dickhead bothered you."

"You know, sometimes I hate how astute you are. The last Master I was involved with didn't need to know such intimate details."

"All that tells me is neither of you were in it for

anything more than a few Dom/sub scenes."

"I'm leaving at the end of May," she reminded him, despite the quick stab of pleasure over the hint he wanted more than that.

"So you keep reminding me. You've got a bite." Pushing to his feet, he helped her up and stood behind her again, helping her reel in her first catch.

Baffled by his attitude, Lisa reminded herself of her life back home. For the rest of the afternoon and on the ride back to the stable, she shored up her resolve to stick to her decision about reaping everything from her limited time with Shawn while she could.

"I can add Walleye to my short list of fish I'll eat. Fresh caught is much better." Lisa took her last bite, enjoying the breeze as they sat out on Shawn's deck finishing dinner.

"My reaction was the same the first time I ate a catch, and I didn't like fish at all at the time. Miss Betty always insisted we try a new food once, no matter how much one of us would balk. Eventually, we did it without fuss just to please her. Split the last roll with me."

He picked up the soft roll from the bakery in town and buttered it, her attention drifting to his long fingers, and how he'd broken through her block, touching her in just the right way. She hadn't figured out yet why his plunging strokes inside her pussy, his pressure against her clit, and his voice in her ear had set her off where Master Wade's same expertise had failed.

"Oh, you go ahead. I'm full," she stated as he held half the roll out to her. "I'll take the dishes inside then get going."

He had grilled vegetables along with the fish, and it was the best meal she could remember eating in a long time, that was what she kept telling herself as he helped clear the table and carry the dishes inside the cabin home. It was better to believe food was the reason for the contented warmth in her abdomen as she'd sat across from him and the burning intensity of his focused gaze for the past hour.

Lisa set the plates next to the large stainless steel sink. The inside of his house mirrored the log structure of the exterior with some walls of smooth, rounded logs and others covered with sheet rock and painted off-white. The high ceiling boasted dark wood beams and low-hanging fans in both the den and dining area, and several large windows let in an abundance of natural light.

"Will you join me at the club tonight?" he asked as she turned from the counter and he took her elbow.

"Sure, but I'll meet you there. I have to change clothes."

A wicked gleam entered his eyes. "I can bring one of my shirts for you to change into."

She liked that idea way too much, since donning his clothing would hint at an intimacy that was neither true nor wise to wish for in a temporary relationship. "Thanks, but then I won't have my car and it's way out of the way to come back here to get it afterward."

"Not if you stay the night."

That idea appealed even more than wearing his shirt, and she tried stepping back from him and the longing to take him up on the offer, but he kept hold of her arm and shook his head. Without his hat, his thick hair fell forward, framing his rugged face.

"If you're not ready, just say so, don't retreat. I thought we had moved past that defense mechanism of yours now that you've reminded me when and where we've met before."

"That doesn't change the fact..."

"Yes, I know," he cut in, displeasure coloring his voice, "you're only here a short time." He started to say something else then obviously thought better of it, huffing in frustration instead. "I'll walk you out, and see you soon, then."

Feeling braver and excited about returning to Spurs for another scene with him, Lisa grinned and went up on her toes to brush a kiss on his corded neck. "I'm looking forward to it."

"So am I."

CHAPTER SEVEN

A vehicle approaching from the direction of Clayton's place snagged Shawn's attention from shutting Lisa's car door, and he stood back as she started for town. He cringed, recognizing Miss Betty's purple Mazda realizing she was close enough to have seen him telling Lisa goodbye. Not that he wasn't always happy to see her, he was. But given her penchant for lecturing them lately to find a good woman and settle down, he knew how she would take to him inviting a female friend to the ranch.

The first day he, Clayton, and Dakota had arrived on Buck's ranch, he'd sat them down and drilled the rules into them. Number one: Show proper respect to his wife, Betty, at all times. Number two: What Betty wanted, she got. The man fucking doted on the woman, and neither he nor she was shy about expressing their love. Clayton was the only one between them raised with both parents, and Shawn remembered seeing sadness darken his friend's eyes when Clayton had first watched the Coopers together.

If it weren't for Miss Betty, as she'd insisted they call her, and her comforting hugs and homemade cooking to soften Buck's gruff, strict control, Shawn doubted neither he, nor Dakota or Clayton would have given her husband a chance to turn them around. Bracing for questions he wasn't ready to ask himself, let alone answer for someone else, he went to help her out as soon as she parked.

Taking her arm as she opened the car door, he zeroed in on the casserole carrier sitting on the passenger seat. "I was going to ask what brings you out today, but I see you're feeding us again. At least, I hope that's for me."

Shawn bent down, and Miss Betty placed a hand on his chest, went up on her toes, stretching her five-foot height to five-foot-two to kiss his cheek. "I think Dakota and Clayton are already digging in, neither happy I didn't stay and join them."

"They forgot it was bridge night, didn't they?" He took the wood handle of the quilted holder, catching a whiff of her mouthwatering enchiladas. "I wish I hadn't just eaten. Damn that smells good. Do you have time to come in and say hi to the dogs? They know you're here."

She smiled, looking toward the side of the house where he'd built the shepherds' dog run. "I see and hear them, and I'm so glad you've finished a safe outdoor space for them while you're away from home. Walk over there with me so I can get going faster, and tell me about the pretty blonde."

"I knew you would ask. Oddly enough, she's someone from my past, was another kid Father Joe stepped in to help. She's only in Mountain Bend until the end of the school year, so don't get any ideas."

Sending him one of her secret smiles that hinted she wasn't buying that was all there was to it, she unlatched the gate and he moved quickly to make sure the exuberant dogs didn't jump on her. She might appear sturdy, and look a decade younger than her sixty-four, but he wouldn't chance her getting knocked down. Curly and Mo had taken to her as fast as they had Lisa.

"If you say so, dear. Hello, boys."

Ten minutes later, Miss Betty looked up at him as she settled behind the wheel again, her hand on the door handle and eyes twinkling. "Bring your girl over for tea and cookies sometime. I'd like to meet a protegee of the good priest."

She closed the door then drove off with a wave, leaving Shawn to question why he hadn't corrected her when she'd called Lisa his girl.

****

Other than pushing her for more than she thought was wise to accept, Lisa was looking forward to spending more time with Master Shawn. She drove home after dinner with giddy anticipation, thinking he was right, now that the secret was out about their brief past, she could stop fretting so much and enjoy the next few weeks, maybe extend her stay if she was needed for summer school. By then, surely her stalker would have forgotten all about her.

Her burst of positive thinking lasted until she returned to her duplex bungalow, through a long hot shower, and while she mulled over what to wear. As she chose a simple ivory camisole to pair with her one denim skirt, her phone beeped with an incoming text. Thinking it might be Shawn, she snatched it off the end table, her eagerness to hear from him changing to a cold knot of dread as she read the message from the one person she never wanted to hear from again.

I'VE FINALLY FOUND YOU. DID YOU MISS ME AS MUCH AS I'VE MISSED YOU?

Hand shaking, she tossed the phone down and cast a frantic look around, as if he was in the room with her. It wasn't until she searched every corner of the entire house and scanned the street for a suspicious vehicle or loiterer that the fear tensing every muscle eased enough for her to take a much-needed breath. She still didn't want to but saw no other choice than to ask Shawn for help, and his protection, even though she cringed imagining his reaction.

Tears pricked her eyes, and she sank down onto the sofa, putting her head in her hands. The distant clap of thunder heralding an approaching storm startled her enough she jumped, raised her head, and searched the shadows in the room. Regardless of what Shawn thought about the nine-year-old girl he once protected showing up in his town twenty years later needing his safeguarding again, she was out of options. She couldn't tell him at the club, though, humiliating herself in public. Even if she had to sleep with one eye open here on the sofa, she could wait one more day to enlist his help.

Returning to the bedroom, she picked the phone up and sent him a quick text, saying only she couldn't make it and would talk to him later. Her gaze landed on the camisole and thong she'd planned to wear tonight, and a spurt of anger shoved aside her fear for a moment. She'd been looking forward to being with Master Shawn again, to submitting to whatever he commanded. He'd come to know her needs well in the short time since they'd reunited, and it grated that she'd finally reached the point of risking further heartache by going for everything she could get only to have the chance stolen from her.

Lisa strode back into the living room, cursing this unknown person who had upended her life. Following her mother's death, she'd been given few choices about her immediate future. The foster family Father Joe recommended had been welcoming and supportive, but she'd missed her mother's love, that extra mile a parent was always willing to go for their child. She'd learned to fend for herself at school, never complain or ask others for help out of fear of ridicule for being a foster kid. Working two jobs and burning the midnight oil for four years to put herself through college had left her too tired or with not enough hours in the day to make friends, date, or party. She'd graduated without forming any close bonds like most college kids did and had been fending for herself for so long, she'd gotten used to not relying on others for help.

A jagged streak of lightning lit up the midnight sky outside the window, the ensuing thunder boom striking much closer and bringing with it a driving downpour. Her nervousness returned, along with the fear, and, to keep herself busy, she retrieved a flashlight, blanket, and pillow and settled on the sofa with the television turned low. Telling herself there was a good chance her stalker had been bluffing and didn't really know where she was, helped calm her anxiety, but the night couldn't pass quickly enough to suit her.

****

Shawn put his beer down to glance at the text from Lisa, his annoyance with her tardiness escalating to anger. Pissed off didn't begin to describe his reaction. *Fuck this.* He wasn't about to let her get away with retreating after they'd come this far. He'd understood her reluctance over revealing their previous connection, but now that they'd cleared that up, he couldn't get a grip on what else she was holding back. Especially after today, when her obvious enjoyment with their outing had shone on her face and come through in her tone all afternoon.

Not to mention the light of expectation in her green eyes when he'd mentioned joining him tonight. For the first time since he'd met her on the road, she hadn't tried to hide her revealing expression, letting him see the vulnerable ache he'd only managed to touch upon relieving last week. He still didn't know what caused the distress that led to her mental block, and that was something he'd planned on addressing tonight.

"Bad news?" Ben asked, cocking his head toward Shawn's phone.

"Nothing I can't handle if I can get away." Shawn scoped out the crowd and activities around the club, noticing all the doors upstairs were closed, the private rooms already fully occupied. The hot tub on the deck held six couples, and Clayton was putting the new fucking machine to good use, keeping a close eye on young Charlotte and the attached dildo slowly plowing her ass. "Excuse me," he told Ben. "I need to check with the guys before taking off. Are you good here?"

"Like always. Anything I can do to help, other than

keep an eye on things?"

"No, but thanks. I've dealt with stubborn subs before, just never one so reluctant to reveal personal issues that need addressing."

Ben chuckled. "I don't envy you the task. Easy-to-please subs are more my preference. I've got enough grief hunting down that fucking bear."

Pausing, Shawn cut him a sharp glance. "Has there been another attack?"

"Only on livestock, and two destroyed campsites, but the son of a bitch left little of the animals, and the campsites looked like a war zone. He is one pissed-off motherfucker, and from the tracks, the biggest I've ever come across."

"Be careful, and give us a call if you need extra scouts."

Catching sight of Dakota coming down the stairs with a woman Shawn didn't know by name, he veered that way, determined not to wait until tomorrow to question Lisa over why she had changed her mind.

"You don't look happy," Dakota remarked as Shawn reached him, the tall brunette sending Dakota a scathing look before tromping off.

"Neither did she...what's her name?"

"Beth, Babs, Barb, something like that."

"Shit, Dakota, can't you bother to get their names right before fucking them?"

Shrugging his massive shoulders, he appeared unconcerned with the girl's attitude. "I usually do, but she pissed me off. Instead of paying attention, I got right down to giving her what she wanted and then ended it. That's the part she didn't like."

"If you don't start giving them more than a

quick scene, or fuck, you'll soon run out of willing partners," he warned, not that it would do any good. Dakota saved all his emotional energy for tracking down his mother's murderer, and had ever since they'd first met.

"Then I'll have more time for other things. What's up with you?"

Giving up, Shawn said, "I need to take off to deal with my girl. Ben's willing to help out if you'll give Clay the message."

"He's a good man. Go." Dakota jerked his head toward the doors. "Storm's coming in fast, so don't delay."

He didn't need further prompting, and Shawn left Spurs, driving into the storm that broke loose halfway to Mountain Bend.

****

Prickles of unease ghosted over Lisa's skin seconds before the lights flickered and went out, along with the television. The storm continued to wage its furious assault, the pounding wind driving the rain against the windows with pelting force, the continuous racket of snapping bolts of lightning and thunderous rumbles enough to keep her nervous tension at a feverish pitch. Searching the sofa under the blanket she'd wrapped around her, she found the flashlight and switched it on.

"Not much help but better than nothing," she uttered out loud, thinking she could use another dose of the anger-infused bravado that had deserted her way too soon earlier.

An eerie sense of foreboding assailed her as she huddled in the dark, listening for sounds other than those coming from the pissed-off skies. Without anything to do, her mind took the path she'd tried to avoid, and she started wondering how her deranged stalker had found her. She'd given up long ago trying to figure out who he was, and what she'd done to earn his attention and hatred.

A creak came from the hall – bathroom, bedroom? Shaking inside and out, Lisa discarded the blanket and gripped the flashlight before standing up and peering down the dark hallway. Another sound, maybe of a window opening, sent her heart into her throat and her feet into motion toward the front door.

"Liiisa."

The whispery voice dragging out her name filtered through the dark and sent her racing outside and into the storm just as headlights turned into the driveway. Soul-deep terror formed a ball of nausea in her abdomen that threatened to come up as she stood undecided in the drenching rain, unable to see who was behind the wheel.

A whimper slid past her constricted throat, and her knees went weak as she watched Shawn unfold his large frame from behind the wheel. She'd recognize that hat and ground-eating stride anywhere and almost tripped over herself to get to him, and safety.

"Lisa!"

"Thank God," she warbled, throwing herself against him, her whole body quaking against his solid strength. "I heard...something...a voice...so scared." She was shaking so hard she couldn't form a coherent sentence, could think of nothing except never letting go.

His arms came around her, righting her world once again, and she simply crumpled, turning into a shaking, garbling, sobbing heap against him.

"*Fuck.*" Pivoting without releasing her, he reached out and opened the passenger door to his cruiser and lifted her inside. "Stay put while I check the house. Lock the fucking door and don't get out until I return."

Shawn's familiar, deep, commanding voice penetrated her shocked senses enough for her to give him a shaky nod. He backed out, the slam of the door rocking the cruiser and galvanizing her into action. Lisa hit the locks, her eyes never leaving his broad back as he sprinted inside the house. What seemed like hours was only minutes later when a vehicle roared down the street behind her, taking the corner with a loud screech that cut through the rolling thunder. She kept her eyes glued to the open front door, waiting for Shawn to reappear. When he didn't return fast enough to suit her frazzled nerves, her mind went down the scariest path of the night.

He's hurt, all because of me. Oh God, what if he's dying, or dead?

She could no more refrain from trying to help him than she could control the weather. Welcoming a return of grim resolve, she pushed the door open against the wind and rain, not bothering to shut it again in her haste to get to Shawn. Fearing the worst sent adrenaline pumping through her blood as she ran inside only to come up against the brick wall of his powerful chest.

"God damn it, I told you to stay put." He clasped her arms, trying to disengage her choking hold.

"You're okay, you're okay," Lisa chanted over and over, refusing to let go as a combination of profound relief and blazing lust changed her body temperature from freezing cold shivers to instant flaming heat. "I thought...are you hurt...I..." She choked, desperate to feel something other than the sheer black fright of the past hour.

"Lisa, everything's fine. He's gone. You're safe."

She shook her head against his damp shirt. *It's not fine because I'll never be safe. He wants me dead. He could have hurt Shawn, or worse...oh God.* Frantic now for a diversion from imagining him dead and to take what she'd wanted from first setting eyes on the man her childhood rescuer had become, she slid down to her knees. The brief flash of lightning outside the window behind her helped her find his belt buckle before the room went dark again.

"Lisa, no, not like this." His hands dropped to her shoulders, the warmth of his palms seeping through her damp shirt. "You're acting on fear...*shit!*"

She smiled as his hot, heavy cock fell into her hands, the tense anxiety of the last hour already starting to fall away. "I'm acting on pure want, Master Shawn," she whispered against his smooth crown.

"Damn it, we need to..." He sucked in a tortured breath, and she swept her tongue over his seeping slit. "*Fuck...*"

"Yes, exactly what I want to do, but not yet." His scent and taste filled Lisa's senses as she swept under the rim of his cock head, teasing the sensitive area then sliding her way down his throbbing shaft.

"Fine," Shawn ground out, his hands lifting from her shoulders to cup her head. Lisa shuddered as he held her still and took over, grateful for his insight about what she really needed right now. His dominant control. "If you regret this, I'll spank your ass until you can't sit down for a week."

If that threat was supposed to give her pause, it failed. The frenzied storm inside her matched the intensity of the one raging outside, and she welcomed the heat of his hard flesh in her mouth wiping away the last tremors of fear. Tightening her hand at the base of his cock, she reached behind him with her free hand and gripped one taut butt cheek, loving the way he held her head immobile and took over by fucking her mouth.

"That's it, Lisa, suck hard, yes, like that...come on now, take a little more."

His guttural tone vibrated above her head, his cock jerking as she accepted another inch and swirled her tongue around his rigid girth, tracing over the bulging, pulsing veins. She moaned around him, and he swore. She scraped her teeth as he pulled back, and he swore. She released her hold on his cock to cup his balls and press his scrotum, and he swore. Lisa locked her lips around his silky cap to keep him from pulling out of her mouth completely, but failed, and she swore.

"Why did you... *Oh!*" she gasped as he grabbed her arms, hauled her up, and pressed her against the wall.

"We're going to have a long overdue talk come morning. Brace yourself."

Shawn ripped off her top and yanked her bra open,

his aggression sending a wild, primitive longing sweeping through Lisa's senses. Her torso was still damp and cold until he put his hands over her breasts, kneading and squeezing before rotating his rough palms over her nipples.

"Yes, sir." She arched into his hands, perspiration pooling on her lower back as slick heat filled her pussy.

Mindless with need, she reached down and undid her jeans with one hand while searching for his straining erection with the other. There was something both intimate and carnal about groping in the dark with only an occasional lightning bolt to provide a shadowy glimpse of his dark face. His breath was hot and heavy against her neck then on her breast as he clamped his mouth around her right nipple.

With a sharp nip that went straight to her empty sheath, he shoved her hands aside and helped free one leg from her jeans. "Lucky for you, I have a condom with me," he rasped, pulling it out of his back pocket and slapping it into her hand.

"Just one?"

His low laugh rumbled from his chest against hers as she ripped it open then worked the thin latex over his cock.

"Now, Shawn, *please*," she begged without shame as she released him.

"Hold on." Grasping her buttocks, he lifted her, and she wrapped her legs around his hips as he worked his way inside her with a slow but relentless push. "Jesus, I forgot how tight you are."

Lisa groaned as he filled and stretched her pussy,

gripping his bulging biceps and wishing she'd thought to at least open his shirt. She craved to touch his bare skin, feel the warmth of his thick muscles under her hands and lips. Then he was grinding into her with deep thrusts that pressed her against the wall and robbed her of coherent thought.

Their breathing turned to harsh pants, the only sound in the room besides the rain beating against the windows to the tune of rolling thunder and the slick merging of his pounding cock burrowing into her wet core. He went deep, bumped her cervix and she whimpered. She shuddered as he circled inside her, teasing the tissues up and down her vagina until stars lit up the darkness behind her closed lids with the first contractions.

"That's it, Lisa." He bit down on her earlobe. "Come for me…yeah, there you go," he breathed against her lips before covering her mouth with his just as she rippled around his ramming cock with an explosion of white-hot pleasure.

Clinging to his arms, hips, and mouth, Lisa gloried in the mind-numbing climax ripping through her body. Impaled against the wall by the strength of his rough possession and massive body, she rode through the storm of untold pleasure, praying it never ended. *This* was what she'd tried to achieve for as long as she could remember, and no matter how he felt about her afterward, this glorious escape from reality into euphoric madness was worth the risk.

Hot licks of pleasure gripped Shawn's cock as he plowed through Lisa's snug, squeezing pussy seconds before his orgasm erupted in a fierce torrent of heat. Flames tore through him as he pumped into her with the rutting intensity of an undisciplined bull. He would berate himself, and her, for that lack of finesse as soon as he returned to sanity. She was the only woman who had managed to strip his control enough for him to trade what he should do for what he'd wanted all along.

He finally regained enough of his senses to slow down and loosen his grip on her ass. Teasing them both by changing his rapid, forceful thrusting to unhurried, in-and-out dips aimed at caressing her still quivering swollen muscles, he kissed her with softer pressure and less demand. By the time the last spasms of his climax abated, their sweat-slick bodies were cooling, reminding him of their damp clothing and how they had gotten wet in the first place.

He muttered a curse and pulled out of her body one final time, releasing her mouth to say, "I've sworn more in the last hour than I did my first month in foster care. Are you all right?" Letting go of her buttocks, he stepped back far enough to give her room to drop her legs while holding onto her hips.

"More than all right. I don't know where to start in thanking you," she replied, her voice breathless and rushed.

"I'll let you know in the morning. Until then" – he reached over and flipped the lock on the front door – "let's turn in. I saw only two bedrooms when I searched the house earlier. Show me which one you're sleeping in."

"You're staying?"

Surprise and relief colored her voice, and he didn't

know whether to pull her close for a reassuring hug or put her over his knee for scaring the hell out of him earlier. Erring on the side of caution, he did neither, instead snatching her hand and pulling her in front of him.

"You couldn't run me off, even if you were foolish enough to try. Crap but it's dark in here."

"First door on the right, across from the bathroom."

"Got it." As they entered the bedroom, the electricity flickered back on, the living room lamp offering enough illumination to find the light switch. "Better." He winced, eyeing the bed. "Only a double, huh? I hope you don't mind being crowded."

"I don't mind. Shawn..."

Placing a finger over her lips, he shook his head, seeing the fatigue and residual fear in her eyes. "In the morning. I'm as wiped as you look." He knew just how emotionally shell shocked with fatigue she was when she didn't argue.

Shawn stripped her of the ruined blouse and bra, making a mental note to replace them. She managed the leg of her jeans on her own while he yanked down the bedspread. "Get in. I'm going to take one more look around."

Lisa padded over, unabashed by her nakedness, and he placed a hand on her butt as she slid under the covers he held up with his other hand. She opened her mouth to say something but clamped it shut again after looking up at him. He didn't doubt his face reflected the turmoil she'd caused him or his resolve to get to the bottom of tonight's break-in.

Pivoting, he left the bedroom and double-checked the front and back doors even though there was no need. He'd been thorough in his search after the perpetrator had taken off through the neighbors' backyards. Not willing to leave her to chase him, he'd swept through the house then hightailed it to the front door where she'd taken years off his life when she'd barreled into him. Nothing could have prepared him for her terrified greeting when he'd first arrived or the gut-wrenching fear and anger he'd experienced hearing her petrified rambling as she shook in his arms.

No one deserved to suffer a traumatizing event once in their lives, let alone twice. The most pressing question he needed answered was if this was a random B&E or something more personal, more sinister. He was tempted to call Father Joe, but he preferred hearing everything from Lisa and didn't want to alarm the priest if this was an attempted robbery. Mountain Bend was a peaceful town, for the most part. They had their bar fights, drunk drivers, wild teenage parties, and domestic abuse, but home vandalism was rare, and given Lisa's reticence toward opening up to him, he couldn't help but think trouble had followed her here.

Returning to the bedroom, he stripped and climbed into the bed, pulling her sleeping form next to him. With him here to protect her, tomorrow would be soon enough to get answers.

****

Lisa awoke from the best night's sleep she could remember getting in months, disappointed when she discovered Shawn's body was no longer wrapped around her, keeping her warm. Then again, all she had to do was think about his rough fucking against the wall last night and his slower, gentler assault on her body in bed hours later to chase away the chill of rolling out of bed. However, with wakefulness came a return of guilt, and regret for the way her silence had inadvertently put him at risk. She'd never wanted to bring her troubles to his doorstep, but sometimes doing what you think is the right thing can return to bite you on the butt.

Spotting his shirt tossed on the floor, she picked it up and slipped it on, enjoying the soft, worn cotton against her skin and the way it dwarfed her smaller frame, much like his hold all through the night. If she wasn't careful, she could get to liking him sharing her bed way too much. She had to keep reminding herself his protective streak was in his DNA, as much a part of him as his rich mahogany hair and gray eyes. Shawn's insistence on sticking around last night had nothing to do with strong feelings for her but more with doing his job as both a cop and a Dom.

With that in mind, Lisa dashed across the hall to use the restroom before following the enticing aroma of coffee into the kitchen. Her heart executed one of those disconcerting flips the moment she saw him leaning against the counter holding a cup of coffee in one hand and his phone to his ear with the other. Her mouth watered as she eyed his bare wide, thick chest and smooth broad shoulders for the first time, recalling the strength in those corded arms as he'd held her pinned to his thrusting hips. She didn't need the sexy look of his unsnapped jeans riding low on his lean hips and emphasizing his six-pack abs to renew a lust that exceeded anything she'd felt before, with anyone else.

First things first before she could entice him into jumping her bones again – a long overdue talk was needed to clear the air.

"Thanks, Dakota, I appreciate the offer. My thoughts exactly. Later."

Shawn clicked off, his gunmetal gaze following her move toward the kitchen island, his jaw tightening as he eyed her bare legs below the shirt's knee-length hem. "Good morning. I helped myself to your kitchen, but all I could find for breakfast was the coffee."

Lisa noticed he didn't apologize for making himself at home, not that she cared. Sucking in a deep breath, she placed her hands on the small island separating them, and blurted, "I'm sorry about last night, and..."

"I hope you're not apologizing for throwing yourself at me and begging me to fuck you. Because that would piss me off."

She gave him a rueful smile. Of all her regrets, that wasn't one of them. "No, you won't get an apology for my panicked pleas. I was talking about not telling you about a stalker I picked up back home and hoped to put off my tail by escaping here for a short time." Her eyes watered, irritating her as he grew blurry for a moment before she blinked them away, refusing to shed one more tear because of that creep.

"How long has this been going on?" Pulling a notepad from his back pocket, he searched for a pen lying around.

"Top drawer behind you. For several weeks before..." Lisa paused as a shudder went through her in remembering how her brakes had failed, and the terror of bringing the careening car under control. "Sorry," she muttered, shaking her head.

"Tell me," he demanded, handing her a cup of creamed coffee across the counter.

After taking a fortifying gulp of sweetened caffeine, she relayed everything she could recall from the first time he contacted her with a hate-filled text up to her failed brakes and enlisting Father Joe's help. Retrieving her phone from her purse by the front door, she handed it to him, glad she'd kept every ugly, nerve-wracking message.

"At least you were thinking straight enough not to delete these." He drilled her with a disapproving glare. "I can't say the same about your thinking since we met again. Care to explain why you didn't come to me right away with this information?"

Lisa's temper shot to the forefront, a defensive reaction, she knew, to her dismay from knowing she'd earned his disapproval. "Get real, Shawn. How would you have reacted if the kid you rescued twenty years ago suddenly showed up at your door and claimed to need your help again? I can just imagine your skepticism." Watching him closely, she saw his hesitation, the look hinting she had a point. "Aha, I'm right, aren't I?"

"Possibly, at first anyway. But not after I took over for Master Simon at Spurs. After that night, you should have revealed everything, if for no other reason than giving a Dom the honesty needed for even a temporary relationship."

His valid point wiped away the edge her comment gave her. That would probably bother her more if she didn't find his bare chest and her memories of all those bulging muscles pressing against her so distracting,

"You're right there," she admitted, sipping her coffee. "My only excuse is I thought my absence had worked since I hadn't heard from him again. That mistake almost got you hurt, and I can never forgive..."

"Lisa," Shawn growled in a sharp tone, his hand slicing through the air. "I'm a trained cop, I wasn't in danger, or even worried. I searched your house with my gun drawn even though I'd heard him running away."

"Gun?" She looked up with her brows furrowed. "I never saw you with a gun."

"You were too frightened when you came in and too out of it after I fucked you to notice I laid it on the nightstand."

He turned slightly, and her eyes slid down his smooth back to the handle of his pistol sticking out of his waistband. "Oh."

"Yeah, oh." Fisting his hands on his hips, he started pacing, shooting questions at her with rapid-fire intensity. "Is there anyone you suspect is doing this to you?"

"No, no one."

"You haven't pissed off a co-worker or close friend?"

"No."

"How about an ex-boyfriend? Someone who didn't want the relationship to end?"

Lisa snorted, shaking her head at the ridiculous idea while trying to clear the lust from her brain. She shouldn't find his aggressive, back-and-forth strides in tight jeans and bare feet and those granite-hard glances he kept tossing her way so arousing. "There were only two affairs, and they broke off with me. I haven't heard from either of them since."

Did he mumble "they were idiots"? No, she must have heard his angry mutter wrong. He stopped pacing to rub his bristled jaw and peer at her with a narrow-eyed look.

"What about at the club you belonged to in Phoenix? A jealous Dom or sub, someone you turned down, or who chose you over another girl, pissing her off? Don't make the mistake of thinking only in male terms as to who it might be."

Was it all the questions she hadn't thought to ask herself before now or the stress of searching her memory banks for a possible suspect that made her ache for him to take her over again? She couldn't think straight with him glaring at her with his wide chest heaving, his tousled hair curling around his neck and probing eyes stirring her blood.

"Lisa."

Her hand shook from the way he growled her name, his eyes going to slits as she pressed her hard nipples against his shirt. Edgy need forced her to tighten her legs together against the dampness threatening to seep out.

"I told you," she said, her voice emerging in a husky whisper, "no one I know would do this. That's the scariest and worse part to deal with, knowing a stranger has targeted me for some obsessed reason.

Shawn."

She stepped forward, ready to beg, but he halted her by taking her arm and turning her toward the counter, using his torso against her back to push her down onto the quartz countertop.

Shawn put his lips against her ear. "Actions, or nonactions in this case, have earned you consequences, not rewards."

His warm breath, soft tone, and veiled threat sent a shiver down Lisa's spine, with goosebumps popping up across her buttocks as he slid one hand between them and caressed her naked cheeks. Her eyes followed his other hand as he reached in front of her to select a wooden spoon from the ceramic utensil holder. Leaning back, he flipped up the shirt and delivered a hard spank to each globe before switching to the spoon. Every tiny molecule in her body burst into flaming sparks as he peppered her backside with blistering swats meant to burn and sting and bring tears of remorse to her eyes.

CHAPTER EIGHT

Shawn stopped belaboring Lisa's ass at six swats with the spoon, the bright red hue covering her rounded globes and her tearful, choked apology enough to satisfy his need to know she wouldn't hold back from him anymore. Tossing the utensil onto the counter, he filled his hands with her hot buttocks and dug his fingers into the soft flesh, enjoying her moan of discomfort and attempt to shift her hips away from his hold.

"No more secrets, Lisa. This bastard means business." A chill swept him as he pictured her struggling to control her car late at night, frantically pumping brakes that wouldn't catch. Fear for her safety had dictated his action as much as a need to ensure she would tell him everything from now on. "In fact" – he released her and helped her upright, turning her to face him as he finished – "you need to stay with me until I catch him."

Taking in her eyes glittering with unshed tears, blonde hair in wild disarray, labored breathing, and flushed face tempted him to offer her a reassuring hug. Not until he got her cooperation though. From the instant denial crossing her face, she wasn't there yet.

"Shawn, I have to get to work in the mornings, not to mention putting you and others on your ranch in harm's way."

"I drive into town for work every morning. You

can ride with me. Whoever this is, he's a coward who doesn't stand a chance if he's stupid enough to come onto our property. Every one of our hired hands carries a rifle to protect themselves and our livestock against predators of all kinds."

She opened her mouth to give him further argument, and he yanked her against him, stopping her with his mouth. By the time he let up and placed his lips over the rapid beat of her pulse in her neck, she was leaning against him with a surrendering sigh.

"I really need to quit losing my backbone when you're around."

For the first time since he'd arrived last night, Shawn's tension eased. Lifting his head, he gave her the smile she deserved. "You showed enough backbone by taking a chance on leaving everything you've ever known in the hopes of freeing yourself from this threat. Now, let me do what I do best, catch the fucker and throw him in jail."

"And if he's let out, then what?"

"If Clayton prosecutes, that won't happen. Anything else, we'll handle. Let's take a shower then go to breakfast. I'm starving."

She sent him a teasing grin as he steered her toward the bathroom. "If we shower together, it'll take longer to eat."

"I can be quick and thorough."

****

Bruce had fumed all the way back to his dingy motel last night, cursing his father and the old man's fucking daughter. He awoke in no better mood as he dressed and went in search of a restaurant capable of serving a halfway decent meal. So far, the culinary pickings in this godforsaken cowpoke part of the country were slim to none. Another thing to blame on his father and Halldor.

He didn't know if she'd managed to get a call in to the police or if a cop just happened by at the perfect time. When he'd sped by the house after his narrow escape, he noticed the official cruiser, and that the lights weren't flashing. Since he never heard sirens, he assumed she'd gotten a call through. Favoring his twisted ankle, thanks to his forced, hasty exit out the bathroom window, he shuffled out to his rental in no mood to wait to strike again. He couldn't return to his luxuries and easy life until he rid himself of the threat Halldor represented to both, and now that the authorities were involved, he couldn't play with terrorizing her first, as was his intention last night.

Itching for action, and her demise, Bruce sucked up his distaste for fast food and picked up a donut and coffee on his return to scout out Halldor's place this morning. He reached the corner to turn onto her street just in time to see her get into the cop's vehicle and get a good look at the cowboy who had fucked up his plans. His size didn't intimidate Bruce – size didn't equate to smarts. Watching them drive off, he wondered if the cop had stayed the night or returned this morning.

Making the turn, he followed at a safe distance for a few blocks, pulling onto a side street as they parked in front of a large home, now a bed-and-breakfast by the sign out front. From the proprietary hand the cowboy placed on Halldor's back and his protective, close bearing as they walked inside, Bruce guessed there was more between them than cop and citizen.

Well, that just sucks. Bruce struggled to get his fury under control, this revelation making his job here much more difficult. He returned to his motel to search his laptop for information on the police force in Podunk Mountain Bend before coming up with another plan to rid himself of the threat to his inheritance. Ending her life didn't bother him, and he was a crack shot with both rifle and pistol but wasn't sure if he could handle *watching* her die. *Fucking bitch.*

****

Shawn returned to town following his Monday morning beat of monitoring traffic and responding to the occasional call, like the one from Gladys Archibald, an eighty-something nosy neighbor. Today, it was those irresponsible Norman teenagers who were coming home late at night, their souped-up cars waking her from a sound sleep. It had taken him the better part of thirty minutes to ensure her he would have a talk with the twin boys about their mufflers. They were good kids, their only vice loud cars. He would take that over drinking and sneaking out any day.

After texting Andi and asking her to clock him at lunch, he parked in front of Clayton's office and honked. He was more than ready for a lunch break and to enlist his friend's advice and assistance with Lisa's stalker. *Shit,* just the word gave him the chills when he thought of someone targeting her.

"Why are you scowling?" Clayton asked, sliding onto the passenger seat.

"Something I want to discuss with you," he answered, veering toward the Watering Hole. Mountain Bend's only bar was a sleazy dive that served up the best damned corned beef sandwich and onion rings within fifty miles. "Food first."

"Works for me, but let me ask this – does it have to do with our temp teacher slash sub?"

"You always were an astute bastard."

"And you were always easy to read. That was her car still parked at your place after eleven last night, wasn't it?"

Shawn reached the bar, parked, and cut the engine, then angled toward Clayton to say, "Yes, and I'm not even going to ask how, or why you know what make of car Lisa drives." Annoyed with the pinprick of jealousy he experienced from Clayton's remark, he slammed out of the cruiser, muffling the idiot's laugh.

"Relax, McDuff," Clayton drawled as he held the bar door open and waved Shawn in ahead of him. "That bright yellow bug is hard to miss in Spur's parking lot, even at night, and I saw her in it shortly after guest night. It's serious, then?"

Shawn nodded toward a corner table in the dimly lit room. Sitting down, he signaled the day waitress, ready to dish out some payback when he saw it was Sharon Mize. Skirting his question, he stated, "I'll never know since she's only here through May. Speaking of serious...afternoon, Sharon."

The thirty-one-year-old, twice-divorced brunette

nodded at Shawn but turned a mega-watt smile on Clayton. "Deputy Sheriff. Hey there, Clayton. What can I get you, darlin'?"

Laying her order pad on the table, she bent over and braced on one arm, holding her pen poised as she locked her gaze on his. Shawn appreciated the blatant view down her gaping, low-cut blouse, even if Clayton didn't from the dark glare he gave her. Clayton made the mistake of dating the woman right after her affair with a married man in Boise ended, going on the rumors she was done with relationships and was only looking for a good time. In other words, perfect for him, until she turned clingy and started hinting at wanting more after a few nights of burning up the sheets.

Two months had passed since Clayton had ended things, but Sharon took advantage of every opportunity to flirt and tempt him into returning to her bed.

"The Monday special, please," Clayton told her.

"Make that two, and two beers," Shawn added.

Straightening up, she ran one long red fingernail down Clayton's arm, her smile suggestive as she replied, "Anything else, you be sure and let me know."

Clayton glared at her back and then at Shawn. "Don't say a word."

"Fine, spoilsport. On to another subject, then. Lisa has picked up a stalker."

"Ah, *fuck.*"

"Exactly." Shawn spelled out what he knew. Clayton might joke around a lot, and had a tendency to take very little seriously, but mention someone getting away with breaking the law, and he could switch from charmer to a ruthless prosecutor without a hitch.

"And she has no clue who this could be?" Clayton asked when he finished.

"None, and I believe her. Now that he's proven he'll chase her down in a different state, she's too worried to hold back, and I drilled her about every relationship, even the ones at the club she frequented in Phoenix. I plan to follow up with Father Joe tonight."

"Keep poking at her for details about everyone she's been in contact with in the weeks prior to the first message. Nine times out of ten, a stalker is someone the victim knows but doesn't have a clue is obsessed. Whatever you need Dakota and I to do, you know we will."

Gratitude filled Shawn. He'd never been more appreciative of the unconditional support they always offered each other. "Thanks. She's staying with me until this bastard is caught, and I'm hoping she'll mention something I can check out."

Sharon returned with their order and provided them with another glimpse down her gaping top as she set the plates down, her suggestive smile and wink only for Clayton. Shawn smirked as Clayton made a point of ignoring her. She reacted to the blatant insult with a huff and twitch of her ass then spun about and stalked over to the next table.

"You've got yourself a real winner, there, pal. I'll bet getting laid wasn't worth the grief of that one."

Clayton's annoyed expression dropped off, replaced by his usual, I-don't-give-a-shit grin.

Picking up his sandwich, he took a huge bite, saying with his mouth chewing, "Not so. I can ignore her, but the dick wants what the dick wants, my friend."

He couldn't argue with that, not when he thought about Lisa. The difference between them being his open mind to more than sex, whereas, Clayton was content and happy to continue playing the field. Neither he nor Dakota were inclined to put out the extra effort needed to form a relationship, or even to hold onto someone for longer than a few bouts of fucking.

"Have you heard old man Sanders finally hired someone to work for him again?" Clayton took a swig of beer, his look turning rueful as he set it down and added, "I wonder how long this one will last?"

The ornery sheep rancher whose property abutted theirs tended to run off the much-needed hands within weeks of hiring them, his crotchety attitude making him too difficult to work for or to spend much time around.

"I'm sure the betting has already started." Shawn's phone beeped as he finished his sandwich, and he answered pushing to his feet, tossing cash down for the tab. "Hey, Kevin, what's up?"

"I could use some backup at the Campbell residence. I'm headed there now," the other deputy sheriff said.

"Shit, not again. I'm leaving the Watering Hole now. Neighbors call it in?"

"Like always. Sounds bad, just so you're aware."

Kevin clicked off and Shawn swore again. One of these days, Chester Campbell would end up killing his wife, Louise, if she didn't stick to at least one of the complaints she tended to file then rescind before the ink dried on her signature.

"I'll ride over with you," Clayton offered as they both dashed out to the cruiser.

"Thanks," Shawn said over the roof of the vehicle, reaching for his door handle. "I may need you to hold me back from laying into that fucker."

"Or," Clayton said, jumping in, slamming the door, and gripping the hand strap above his head as Shawn peeled out with the siren blaring, "I could lend you a hand."

One look at Louise as he stormed into their house, and Shawn hoped the ambulance was en route. He barely recognized her face, and the odd angle of her shoulder explained why she was cradling her arm against her waist where she huddled over on the sofa. Chester, a big brute of a man, struggled in Kevin's hold, his face a drunken, mottled red, his voice laced with vitriol as he ranted against his worthless wife and cursed their interference. The same crap he spewed every time he got drunk and lost his temper.

"I'll see to her." Clayton didn't wait for his nod before squatting in front of Louise to assess her injuries.

Shawn stormed across the worn carpet just as Chester broke free from Kevin. *You bet, fucker. Take a swing at me.* He braced for the older man's attack, shifting his torso as Chester swung so his fist smacked nothing but the air. Grabbing his wrist, Shawn jerked him around by the arm and shoved him against the wall hard enough to fell two photos. He put all of his weight against Chester's flabby body, smashing the side of his face against the peeling paint with another upward wrench of his arm behind him.

"This time" – Shawn yanked Chester's arm up another notch – "you've really done it. You're getting locked up, and staying locked up if I have to lose the key to keep you there."

"This is between me and my old lady. Fuckin' cops got no business buttin' in a man's affairs with his wife, I'm gonna....*aaagh!*" Chester wailed as Shawn's next twist upward on his arm popped the shoulder joint. "I'll...s...sue!" he gasped.

Shawn looked at Kevin, who stood next to them and said, "I didn't see anything."

"Me either," Clayton called out as he went to the door to wave the paramedics inside, his expression a mask of stone.

Shawn released his bruising hold and clamped restraints on Chester's wrists, suspecting Clayton hadn't gotten a lot of cooperation from Louise. After learning the drunk driver who had killed his parents in a hit-and-run car accident not only possessed a long record of arrests for DUIs but had once again been let go on a technicality, he'd made it his life's work to put criminals away and to keep them there.

Signaling the third paramedic to enter the house, Shawn jerked a thumb at Chester. "Check his shoulder before we transport him, will you, Michael?" he asked, recognizing the young man whose brother worked for them on the ranch.

"Sure thing, Deputy Sheriff. It looks like you've taken a nasty fall, Mr. Campbell."

Leaving Kevin in charge, Shawn followed the gurney holding Louise out to the ambulance with

Clayton, feeling better. "No luck?"

"Some but not enough. That's why I plan to get my car and make a pest of myself until she understands this time and agrees to file charges without dropping them."

"All we can do is keep trying."

Shawn returned to the office, unable to keep from picturing Lisa suffering at the hands of a bully and coward, like Louise. Unlike the battered woman he'd just left, Lisa had been willing to take drastic steps to protect herself. He could admire her for that while, at the same time, it still rankled she had held back from him until she found herself in jeopardy again. This time around, he would leave Louisa's case in Clayton's hands so he could expend all his energy protecting Lisa and stopping a stalker.

****

Friday afternoon, Shawn pulled up in front of Dale's Western Wear to pick Lisa up, his frown telling her he was still chafing from her insistence on shopping before they drove back to the ranch. She'd hitched a ride from Kim and Debra as they were leaving school, the two teachers she'd come to know the best since the night she'd taken in a movie and dinner with them. As much as she loved staying with him, and spending every night in his bed, his insistence on driving her in every morning instead of following her, and the waiting around at school for him to pick her up when she could get a ride with someone else was starting to grate.

Between the tension of waiting for her stalker

to strike again and Shawn's rigid rules causing questions from her co-workers she didn't want to answer, she was just as on edge with his help as she'd been when coping alone. With luck, whatever scene he put her through tonight at Spurs would help.

Shawn pushed open the passenger door, eyeing her large bags with a raised brow. "Did you buy out the store?"

"No, but two items are good-sized," she answered, leaning over the seat to toss them in the back. "And, no, you can't see them until we leave for the club tonight."

Pulling away from the curb, he dropped a bombshell on her. "We're not going this weekend. It's best to lie low until I get a lead on this guy. I've hit dead ends with the report I got from foster care and researching your mother's background."

Lisa went rigid with anger and disappointment. "I would be as safe at the club as I am at your place, probably safer with so many people around. He'd have to be crazy to try anything there."

"Most stalkers are crazy," he shot back. "And unpredictable. I've already mentioned it to Dakota and Clayton, and they have no problem running things without me. Ben and Simon will help."

"Oh, well, as long as *they* agree, then far be it from me to argue over what I want."

"Sarcasm doesn't suit you," he said, giving her a disapproving glare.

"Neither does sitting around all night."

She fumed in silence the rest of the way, and he let her until he parked and turned to her with a Dom's scowl. "I can always give you what you're pining for here at home."

Suppressing the wave of heat his comment ignited, she flung open the door, reached behind the seat for her purchases, and lied. "I'm not in the mood anymore."

He didn't respond as he followed her inside, didn't say a word about it as they greeted the dogs. While they made spaghetti together he told her about the Campbells' history of domestic violence and his hope this time would end differently for Chester. When he went out with the dogs after they did the dishes without mentioning her disgruntled remark, she suspected he was planning a retaliation.

Like always, Lisa's body betrayed her, reacting to all the possibilities running through her head with soft pulses between her legs and tingling nipples. "I said I'm not in the mood," she mumbled under her breath, glancing out the window above the sink and watching him throw a ball for Mo and Curly, her chest tightening when his deep laugh filtered through the open window. He was as diligent in caring for the neglected dogs as he was with her safety, and she couldn't fault him for that. She also couldn't continue under such confined conditions because that wasn't living and meant the bastard who was after her had already won.

Shawn wouldn't see it that way, and she refused to give in, no matter how much she longed to, or how edgy with suspicion and need she grew because he refused to mention her retaliation. Keeping her guessing was a sneaky Dom's ploy she'd never experienced before. To take her mind off him, she changed into the pair of loose shorts and tank top she often wore to bed when at home, planning to leave them on instead of joining him in bed later naked, then went to find something on television to occupy the time.

"What are you watching?" he asked, coming into the den an hour later.

Lisa looked up at him from where she sat curled in the corner of the sofa, her heart flipping as she took in his wind-blown hair, deep breathing, and taut stretch of the tee shirt he'd changed into when they got home. Did he have to pack such a wallop every time she saw him?

She forced her pout into a teasing grin as she replied, *"While You Were Sleeping,"* knowing how much he disliked chic flicks.

He snorted with derision. "I'll leave you to finish it, then, and get some work done in my office."

Left alone to stew in a situation of her own making, the movie, one of her favorites, failed to distract her from wanting the very thing her burst of temper denied her. When Shawn still hadn't emerged from his office after the movie ended, she sat through another Sandra Bullock feature, ready to cede the battle by the time she turned off the television two hours later.

She gave the dogs a bedtime treat then padded down the hall, jumping when Shawn opened his office door as if listening for her. "Ready to turn in?"

"Yes." She waved a hand inside the office. "But feel free to continue working. Good night."

The wicked gleam she'd come to learn could mean anything entered his eyes as he clasped her hand and tugged her down the hall toward his room.

"Now, what kind of Dom would I be to let you go to bed without addressing the challenge you tossed out earlier?"

Despite the humor lacing his voice and the quick surge of arousal simmering through her veins, her palms turned sweaty from apprehension. "I don't know what you're talking about. All I said was I wasn't in the mood tonight."

"Ah, but that was a lie, wasn't it? Never mind, you don't have to answer since I know it was." He gestured toward the attached bathroom in the master bedroom. "Go ahead, but come out naked."

"What if I'm still not in the mood?"

"One" – he flicked a turgid nipple outlined by the thin tank – "you'd be lying again. Two, you have a safe word – use it if you're serious."

No can do, not after that light touch almost – set her off. *I really didn't think this through*, she admitted as she pivoted and strode into the bathroom, closing the door behind her. She took her time, hoping to grow a backbone against her traitorous body, but when his deep voice, vibrating with impatience, reached her through the door and liquid heat filled her pussy, she gave up.

"Lisa."

Opening the door, she padded across the plush oatmeal-colored carpet, her entire body going cold then hot when she spied the dual bullet vibrators in his hand.

"Have you used these before, then?" he asked, drawing her forward when she stumbled to a stop.

"No, but I know what they are. I've never been much for toys."

"Because you prefer jumping straight into the core of a scene instead of taking your time getting there, cutting off any chance to build a connection. Your previous Masters shouldn't have allowed that. Lie down, knees bent and spread."

Lisa settled into position on the bed, ignoring Shawn's astute deduction, caving to the need for his touch again. The cool air wafting in from the slightly open window chilled her heated flesh as she spread her bent knees, but his potent, hot gaze on her gaping labia was all it took to heat her up again. Fisting her hands, she shifted under his silent stare until he raised his eyes to her face and stilled her restless movements with nothing more than a molten stare.

"Better, now don't move," he ordered, lubing the anal vibrator with its nubby nodules as opposed to the smooth rubber of the attached vaginal probe.

"Easy for you to say," she gasped as he worked the bullet into her butt with slow twists and pushes.

He answered her remark with a sharp smack on her thigh that burned then throbbed, much the same as her anus by the time the toy lay embedded inside her untried orifice.

"Lisa."

She sighed, loving that dark tone, and how he didn't need to use endearments, just her name, for her heart to execute that little flip that indicated she was in peril of losing it to him altogether.

"From the snug fit, I'm guessing you haven't indulged in much anal play or sex," he commented casually, sliding the other bullet into her pussy with slick ease, his eyes never leaving her face.

Staving off the urge to squirm as her breath caught

from the instant grip of pleasure circling the toy, she managed to get out the expected reply. "No, that's never been my thing."

"*Mmmm*, we'll have to see about that."

Picking up the remote, he flicked it on, and tiny pulsations erupted inside both channels. The teasing, stimulating repetition along sensitive tissues she never imagined she possessed were impossible to ignore, let alone not respond to with sweeping arousal. Shawn pulled the covers farther down and waved a hand for her to slide under. With the inferno already erupting in her pussy and butt with as much heat as an Arizona desert, she welcomed the cool caress of the sheets he flipped over her.

Shawn stripped, turned the light off, and joined her in his bed, pulling her against him with a gruff, startling command followed by switching off the vibrators. "Go to sleep."

Payback's a bitch. Whoever coined that phrase had it right. Fuming, her body still pulsating, Lisa knew it would do her no good to gripe about his punishment. Sucking up the discomfort, she huffed and closed her eyes, letting his steady heartbeat under her head lull her to sleep. A second before she dropped off, the vibrators started up again, humming inside her with intense waves of pulsating pleasure that went on and on, until her climax hovered, just out of reach then was removed altogether with the abrupt cessation of arousing massages.

"Shawn," she groaned his name in complaint, pressing her mound against his granite-hard, hair-roughed thigh, seeking relief.

"Go to sleep and behave."

"Is that all you have to say?"

"Yes."

Lisa awoke out of sorts, with her pussy and anus still tingling even though Shawn had removed the vibrators after another two rounds of orgasm-denial torture in the middle of the night, leaving her teetering on the razor-sharp edge of climax. She stumbled into the bathroom, glad for once he was such an early riser and already out of the room. The temptation to kick him might prove impossible to deny given her mood.

After taking a long shower, she went in search of coffee and Shawn but only found the coffee and a note from him waiting for her in the kitchen. "Smart man," she uttered, reading he would return to pick her up for lunch with Dakota and Clayton. After downing two cups of coffee and a piece of toast, she played with the dogs before sitting down in the kitchen to work on midterm grades, happy to note how well all her students were doing.

Shortly before Shawn said he'd return, she shut down her laptop and went to change into the short denim-flared skirt, cowgirl boots, and hat she'd bought yesterday. The forecast promised temperatures over sixty today, and she hoped they would sit outside to take advantage of the warm spell.

Speaking of warm spells, she mused, eyeing Shawn entering the house carrying a small bag, a light of appreciation in his gaze as he took in her bare legs. "Hi. I'm ready."

"Nice, and a good choice." Holding up the bag, he came toward her with that wicked gleam that always curled her toes and put her on alert. Taking her hand, he tugged her into the den and over to the sofa. "Bend over so I can insert your new butt plug before we leave."

Without giving her time to think that through, he guided her down, and she braced on her hands, a flush stealing over her face as he lifted the skirt and lowered her panties. She sucked in a breath as he pressed the bulbous, smooth end of the greased plug past her tight resistance, preparing for the discomforting tightness and stretch that had accompanied the new-to-her ripples of pleasure that sexually neglected part of her anatomy was capable of producing.

"You expect me to sit through lunch with this thing?" she asked as he helped her upright and the full impact of the bigger device left her quaking.

"You'll be fine for a short time. You can use Dakota's restroom to remove it after we eat. He just texted and said burgers will be ready soon, and I worked up an appetite checking our irrigation system this morning, so let's go." He pulled up her panties and ushered her out the door.

Lisa grabbed the hat that matched her boots off the entry table then barely managed to get through the ten minute drive over a dirt road without either clobbering him or reaching under her skirt to get herself off. She was quite proud of her restraint by the time they reached Dakota's place and the main hub of the ranch's buildings and activity. Shawn came around, lifted her down from the high cab and set her down, the light impact of her feet touching the ground enough to shift the plug.

As he took her hand and they walked around the side of the house, she sought to distract herself from the riot of sensations every step stirred up by pointing to a smaller structure surrounded with fencing. "What do you keep in there?"

"That's a chicken coop. The ones not inside nesting are roaming now. They all get penned at night."

She took in the two-story, barn-shaped coop with windows and perches. "Lucky chickens. I never knew they made them so big and nice."

"Just a matter of keeping them safe and happy to either lay eggs or become dinner."

She winced. "Oh, not so lucky then."

Shawn chuckled and squeezed her hand. "You've got to toughen up if you're going to hang around a ranch, city girl."

More like she would have to harden her heart in order to return home with it in one piece. Warmth spread from her butt to her pussy and up to her face as she glanced from Shawn's rugged profile to Dakota and Clayton, who were already seated at the outdoor table, wondering how she would keep her feelings hidden during lunch.

CHAPTER NINE

Shawn leaned back in his chair and sipped his iced tea, smiling to himself as Lisa shifted on her seat and tried to hide a grimace from Dakota and Clayton. He imagined the plug was starting to get uncomfortable, and checked the time. A few more minutes and he'd remind her to use the restroom before they went riding. Even with dealing with the distracting toy, she managed to fend off Clayton's teasing barbs and wasn't intimidated by Dakota's quiet, somewhat aloof attitude.

He understood why she was chafing at his restrictions, why she'd gotten ticked last night when he announced they weren't going out to the club. Having her life upended again by a stranger hell-bent on terrorizing her for some unknown reason was upsetting; he got that. But unlike her annoyance, she failed to hide the fear her stalker's return caused, and those unguarded looks shored up his resolve to ensure nothing happened to her.

Her little retaliation of announcing she wasn't in the mood had both amused him and pissed him off, and his initial reaction was to give her a harder, longer punishment spanking. Remembering the plans he harbored for that ass, not to mention the desire to take her out for another ride, he'd nixed that idea. The orgasm denial he'd put her through was working just as well, from the frustrated consternation flashing in her eyes. At least it took her mind off her fear for a while.

As Dakota steered the conversation toward Lisa's troubles, Shawn took the last bite of his burger, wishing he could have kept her smiling and relaxed a little longer.

"Shawn says you can't come up with anyone who has reason to want you dead," Dakota stated with his usual bluntness.

"Jesus, Dakota, can't you at least try subtlety once in a while?" Clayton admonished when Lisa paled.

"Why?"

Clayton rolled his eyes at the blunt, obtuse reply and looked to Shawn to take over. Before he could say anything, Lisa shook her head, color seeping back into her cheeks.

"No, and I've tried, racked my brain now for weeks, and can't come up with a single person, or even an incident that warrants checking into. I'm sorry."

"It's not your fault," Shawn assured her. "He wants you to think it is, wants you upset and not thinking straight to make it easier for him to not only act but get away with his crime."

"How about your mother, Lisa? Can you recall anything she said about your father? I know she left his name off your birth certificate, but did she ever mention him at all, even in passing?" Clayton asked.

"Not that I remember, but I was only nine when she died. I can vaguely recollect her saying once we didn't need his money to get by, that she could take care of me without his help, or maybe it was Mrs. Wilcox she said that to, the elderly woman in the apartment next to ours who stayed with me at night while Mom worked. If she said that, I don't know if it was in reference to him not paying child support or to having money, but either way, that wouldn't make any difference. If he didn't care enough about either of us back then, he wouldn't now."

Lisa's calm voice matched her expressionless face as she nibbled on chips, her blasé attitude indicating she didn't care about the man one way or another. Shawn understood that well; he'd never given much thought to his absentee mother and couldn't miss what he'd never had.

Dakota nailed Shawn with a black-eyed glare. "You find the fucker and give me five minutes with him. You'll have your answers. I've got work to do. You two clean up."

He stalked away, heading to the stables without another word, and Shawn grinned at Lisa's puzzled expression as she said, "I thought he didn't want to get involved."

"Dakota's all about getting revenge. He usually saves his energy for finding whoever murdered his mother, but once in a while, he'll remind us he's not as cold as he comes across," Shawn replied.

"You wouldn't seriously let him..."

Clayton laughed and shucked her under the chin. "No, darlin', we wouldn't, but that look on your face would tempt a saint into coming to your defense." He gave her hair a playful tug, asking, "Are you sure you don't have a sister since Shawn has already laid claim to you?"

"What?" Her startled gaze flew to Shawn.

Shawn liked the idea of claiming her way too much to dispute Clayton, so instead, he changed the subject, noting the time. "Lisa, use the restroom before we go riding." When her eyes turned frosty, he realized his mistake in making that sound like an order instead of a reminder about removing the plug.

Standing, she snatched her hat off the table and plopped it on her head. "I think I'll go hang out with Angel while you two take care of the table."

With that rebuff of his remark, she spun about and trounced across the yard, both men's eyes drawn to her butt twitching in the short skirt. As they stood, Shawn responded with a primitive urge to stake that claim Clayton mentioned.

"Excuse me, but I have a more pressing matter to see to right now."

Donning his own hat, he stomped after her as Clayton said in reminder, "Dakota's in that stable."

"What's your point?" he returned without slowing or looking back.

"Perv," Clayton called out with a snicker.

Maybe I am, he admitted but thought it was more that he wanted what he wanted, and he wanted Lisa. With his blood pumping hot and fast through his veins, Shawn entered the stable and looked toward Dakota, who stood grooming Phantom's coal-black mane and tail. The darker coloring stood out against the Morgan's dark-gray coat, the huge stallion a stunning horse that always drew eyes. With a jerk of his thumb toward the rear, Dakota indicated Lisa's whereabouts.

Shawn lifted his hand and traveled the wide brick aisle between stalls with ground-eating strides, his cock already full and aching to sink into her tight, wet pussy. He remembered the plug, and damn near spewed his seed imagining the extra snugness it would create. Her little snit was working in his favor.

Rounding the corner, he spotted her bending over next to the apple barrel, reaching for a dropped apple. Without pause, he strode forward, grabbed her hips, and nudged her feet apart with one booted foot.

"You know, Lisa, for someone with your experience, you've been awful defensive to your Dom lately. Grab your ankles and hold tight."

"Shawn!" she squealed as he flipped up her skirt and yanked down her panties to reveal her plugged ass and creamy, glistening slit.

Keeping hold of her right hip, he ran a finger through her damp folds. "You were saying?" he asked as she sucked in a breath and groaned.

"What...what if someone comes...in?"

She knew Dakota was already inside, so she was referring to other ranch hands. He remembered her penchant for exhibitionism with a slow smile. Confident Dakota would keep everyone else out, he pumped three fingers inside her pussy, loving the quick grip of her muscles and added tightness, omitting that tidbit from his reply. "Since there's always that chance, I'd better hurry." Pulling out of her sheath, he ripped open a condom with his teeth and made short work of freeing his throbbing erection.

"I'm glad you ignored common sense for once and didn't remove the plug," he said, working his cockhead through the narrow gap of her labia. With short, repeated jabs inching in deeper each time, he labored without pause until he slid home with a final push. *Home*. That's the right term for what he felt every time he was inside her.

"*Oh!*"

Pulling back, he ground out, "Is that a good oh, or bad?"

"Good, Sir, so good."

Hell, yeah, she's mine. A few more strokes and her pussy stretched to accommodate him with the plug, leaving him free to plunder her depths with the rigorous fucking they both craved.

Lisa's head swam from both the upside down position and the escalating arousal Shawn's pussy-invading thrusts were igniting. His tight grip on her hips helped anchor her, leaving her free to concentrate on the fast-building pleasure sweeping her senses. She thought of how fast she'd switched from disappointment to anger when he'd bypassed Clayton's assumption she was his and casually instructed her to use the restroom, referring to removing the plug. Had she known another bout of rough sex would occur, this time with the smell of hay, leather, and horses surrounding her and one of his best friends a few feet away, she would have skipped lunch and headed out here sooner.

The relentless tension of unfulfilled arousal built to an aching crescendo, the hours of orgasm denial he'd put her through responsible, in part, to her fast, cock-hugging response as soon as he'd crammed his thick erection inside her. Discomfort from the packed fullness of the dual penetration heightened her arousal, her nipples contracting so tight they hurt, feeding fuel to the fire raging below, or in this position with her butt elevated upward of her torso, above. Nothing mattered but the pounding together of their hips, the forceful thrusts of his steely cock invading her welcoming pussy, and a euphoric end to the torment of being kept on edge for hours.

If it weren't for Shawn's hold, Lisa's knees would have buckled as her climax exploded in a bright flare of heat and powerful contractions kneading his cock and the plug. She lost track of time and place as he ground into her over and over, every ripple of her muscles releasing more sparks of pleasure. He grunted and held her hips still as he orgasmed, the telltale tremors of his flesh against her sensitive tissues producing another round of answering quivers within her body.

By the time he pulled both his cock and the plug from her well-used orifices then lifted her to wrap an arm around her waist and snuggle her back against his front, nestling his shaft between her cheeks, nothing mattered except these few moments of enjoying the aftershocks of his possession in his arms.

****

"I'm surprised Shawn agreed to this given his watchdog attitude," Jen said as Lisa settled on the passenger seat of her car and shut the door.

Thinking of Shawn's retaliation over the weekend for her snippy mood his hovering had precipitated produced tingles down her spine. Here it was, Wednesday, four days later, and she still quivered when she recalled the raw carnality of their coupling in the stable and the tight squeeze he didn't let deter him from taking her fast and furious. Her imagination had been running amok with other possible places and scenarios on his ranch where he could take control of her.

"I doubt he would have if he could have gotten off work this afternoon, but his boss called in sick, putting him in charge, and I flat-out refused to hang around the station all afternoon. I'm just glad you could get away."

With conferences scheduled for Thursday and Friday, school had closed at noon today to give teachers a chance to work on grades. When she'd told Shawn Jen was free for lunch and had invited her to go sightseeing at the nearby ghost town, he couldn't argue when she'd pointed out there was safety in numbers. The area had seen an increase in visitors with the spring opening of the popular tourist attraction and start of turkey hunting.

"He didn't tell you?" Jen asked, driving toward the deli they'd agreed on for lunch.

"Tell me what?"

"Shawn called Drew and asked him to accompany us today. He'll meet us after lunch, though, since the last guest to check in doesn't arrive until twelve-thirty."

"I should have known his compliance was too good to be true, not that I don't like Drew," Lisa added hastily, realizing how that sounded.

Jen laughed and gave her a quick glance. "I get it. We love 'em, but also want our girl time, or alone time."

"Oh, it's not like that with us." *Love*? She couldn't

afford to fall in love with Shawn, even though she was halfway there already. And he'd never said a word about wanting anything more than a temporary relationship, despite his possessive, caring attitude of late, not even when Clayton had given him the perfect opening the other day.

"If you say so. Just remember, I've known Shawn a long time, and I've never seen him so taken with anyone. And believe me, he's had his choice since high school." Jen parked in front of the deli and grabbed her purse. "Come on. All this talk about guys has my stomach growling."

"For food?" Lisa asked as they entered and veered toward the only vacant table left.

"I'm always hungry for other things, but, yes, food. Oh, good, Hattie made her German potato salad today."

Jen went to get their order while Lisa held the table for them, greeting people she knew as they came in and walked by. Every time she went someplace in Mountain Bend now, she recognized townsfolk she'd talked to or become acquainted with in the last month. She was even getting good at picking out the visitors: who was a tourist passing through as opposed to a year-round resident. The slower-paced way of life in small-town America had grown on her, so different from maneuvering through traffic to work and shop in a city as big as Phoenix, the population too large to offer many chances for a random meeting with a friend.

She'd grown closer to Jen in this short time than she'd bonded with anyone else, either at the Phoenix club or school, maybe because she'd never cultivated a friendship with anyone in the lifestyle. She liked having someone she could hang out with and not have to watch everything she said, someone who understood why submitting worked for certain people and didn't judge.

Lisa thought of Father Joe and how much she missed him, then imagined how much she would miss Shawn when she returned home. With a pang, she realized her feelings for her childhood rescuer were already entrenched deeper than was wise.

"What are you thinking about that makes you look so sad?" Jen set a tray down and took a seat.

"Nothing other than wishing whoever is after me would get tired of his game." Jen and Drew were the only ones she'd told about her stalker, and that was because she had to let them know why she wouldn't be at the house for a while, and that they should keep an eye on their property. She'd expected Shawn to mention it to Dakota and Clayton in case the trouble followed her out to their ranch. "I really appreciate you and Drew taking off for me today."

"You bet. We've got your back, girlfriend, but I have no doubt Shawn will find this perv. Now, perk up and try that potato salad, you'll love it."

The Rueben and salad did help, and Lisa managed to put aside the melancholy that threatened her mood by the time they left to meet Drew.

****

Bruce couldn't believe his luck had finally changed when he happened to see Halldor exiting the deli up the street from where he'd parked in front of the gun shop. It had taken a week of furtive, limited surveillance to figure out she was staying at the sheriff's ranch, and what a huge kink that put in his plans. From what he'd seen, and learned about Deputy Sheriff McDuff, he wasn't a man to mess with. He'd spent time mapping out the route they took from her school and the station and the drive to the ranch, unable to come up with a way to get to her. With his patience shot to hell and his temper a hair-trigger away from exploding, he made the snap decision to follow her when he didn't see her watchdog anywhere around.

Malicious glee filled him as the two women drove past the city limits, but he held back from running them off the road with all the traffic. When they pulled into a parking lot down by the river, and he noticed the old buildings, he groaned in frustration. *Now I have to wait while she plays tourist?* Yet one more delay to piss him off further, his anger increasing when a man joined them and they walked toward the entrance of the old mining town together. If he had his way, Lisa Halldor would join the ghosts haunting the one-hundred-fifty-year-old buildings today.

****

What was I thinking? Shawn gave up trying to fill out reports in favor of listening to his sixth sense that always told him when something wasn't quite right. Since everything here at the station was calm and quiet, and his uneasiness began at noon when Lisa called to say she was with Jen, as he'd asked, he heeded his instincts. Striding out to his cruiser, he whipped out of the parking space and sped out of town, toward the river ghost town.

Lisa followed Drew and Jen out of the century-and-a-half-old saloon, sipping the last of a sarsaparilla as they walked down the boardwalk toward the exit. Touring the old mining town had been a fun diversion from worrying about a crazy person. The buildings alone spoke of the history without a tour guide reciting a prepared monologue. She didn't need to see or even believe in ghosts to get a chill when Drew led the way through the incredibly preserved buildings, telling her about the terrible confrontations that had erupted between the miners and mining companies, many ending in violence and death.

"So, you learned all that in high school history, and actually remember everything? I'm impressed," she told Drew as they wound through the parking lot toward their cars.

"Don't be. He's a history buff and continues reading everything he can get his hands on, especially books about Idaho's past." Jen tossed her bottle into a recycle bin as they reached the back row.

"What can I say? It's a lot more interesting than current events."

The loud rev of an engine caught her attention as Lisa stepped away from her friends to walk around to the passenger side of Jen's car. Pausing in the lane, her heart jumped to her throat seeing the approaching car speed up and aim right for her. Drew's shout reached her as she started to jump out of the way, but the body-slam of a familiar build propelled her on top of the trunk, and she landed with Shawn's heavy weight pinning her down, his labored breathing and low curses ringing in her ears.

"Fuck, Shawn, he came out of nowhere!"

Lisa caught Drew's face out of the corner of her eye as he glared toward the vehicle roaring away. "Shawn, you're crushing me so I...can't breathe."

He swore again and lifted off her, both him and Drew taking her arms to help her stand, which was a good thing given her wobbly legs and shocked state of mind. Tears pricked her eyes even though she wasn't hurt. The very idea someone wanted her dead, hated her to that extent without knowing why, not only left her terror stricken but grieved in a way she'd never experienced before.

"Why, Shawn?" she whispered in a tremulous voice. "Why is he doing this?"

"I don't know, Lisa, but I won't let him get away with it, I promise."

His rough tone carried a note of grim resolve, and she could almost feel his fury as he held her close. She shouldn't count on his promise, but hearing it helped ease her tremors and her mind.

"I believe you." Pulling away enough to look at his face, she asked, "What are you doing here anyway?"

"He probably didn't trust me to watch out for you, which turned out to be a good thing." Disgust laced Drew's voice. "I tried to get the license but the plate was covered with mud."

"On purpose, no doubt," Shawn returned. "You were right there, Drew, and would have saved her from serious injury if I hadn't cut you off. Don't beat yourself up over what that asshole's doing."

Jen squeezed her husband's arm. "Shawn's right, you were on top of the danger immediately. Lisa, are you sure you're okay?"

"Yes, still digesting how fast that happened, but I'm not hurt. Thank you, all of you."

"You can thank me after I lock the bastard up and throw away the key. Come on, let's go home. Jen, Drew, we'll get in touch later."

Bruce vibrated with rage as he saw Halldor clinging to the deputy sheriff and knew where the couple would go next. Determined to end this now, without further delay, he kept driving until he reached the turnoff for the back road they would take to the ranch. If he moved fast enough, he could set up in the woods several yards from the road, cocked, aimed, and ready to fire. This time, he wasn't taking any chances on failing, and if her bodyguard got in the way, he'd take him out along with Halldor and the threat she posed to his way of life.

Shawn couldn't recall a time in his life when he'd been so terrified. As he got on the road back to the ranch, he couldn't keep from checking on Lisa, just quick glances to ensure she was all right. In the split second he'd seen that car coming around the bend into the last row in the parking lot where she stood with Drew and Jen, he only had time to register the threat before leaping from his SUV to rush forward.

Whoever this person was, he was hell-bent on taking her out, for whatever reason had gotten into his warped head. Not trusting anything to chance, he shifted on the seat to reach his cell and press Dakota's number while maintaining a constant eye out for someone tailing them. As soon as Dakota answered with his usual clipped greeting of "What's up?" Shawn gave him the rundown.

"Who do you have close enough to the road to watch for a muddy blue sedan?"

"Pete and Casey for sure. I'll check in with Dave and Scotty. Hang tight."

Dakota clicked off, leaving Shawn confident he would have their backs if this prick was foolish enough to come after Lisa again today.

"I'm proud of you, Lisa. A lot of women would be in hysterics right about now." He sped past a herd of buffalo who often grazed on their land near one of the watering holes, one reason why they left the majority of acreage unfenced.

"I've had a lot of practice at keeping calm lately," she returned dryly.

He appreciated her attempt at humor, not at all sure he could handle her tears right now if she fell apart. Reaching across the gearshift, he squeezed her hand, noting the coolness of her skin and pale face. "We'll figure out who it is and get him. Clayton is still researching your background, and he's good at digging out information."

"I'm grateful for his efforts but hate I've brought this to you and your friends. This is exactly what I didn't want in coming here, to impose on you, or become a burden."

She turned her head toward the window with a sigh that made him want to rip this guy's heart out. He looked her way again and went rigid when he caught a bright flash from a small, wooded area. Slamming on the brakes, he whipped the cruiser around with a shout.

"Get down!"

With a startled cry, Lisa threw herself to the floor as he came to an abrupt, jarring halt with his side door taking the bullet. Grabbing his rifle from above them, he flung his door open and jumped behind it, taking aim over the window.

"Stay down," he barked when she started to rise right as the next bullet caught him in the shoulder.

"Shawn!"

"No." He spared a precious second to address her stricken gasp and reassure her. "It's just a flesh wound, Lisa."

Lisa's stomach churned with nausea from the bright red stain spreading across Shawn's khaki shirt before a reverberating roar of engines and pounding hooves snagged her attention. Peeking over the dash, she saw two trucks barreling across the field and coming to rest at each end of the clump of trees that hid her attacker. The two cowboys in each vehicle flung open their doors and mimicked Shawn's stance, crouching behind them, rifles aimed toward the woods.

"Fucking fool," she heard Shawn mutter.

Cutting her gaze toward the road, she gasped watching Dakota ride toward them, shocked to see him maintaining his seat on the massive, galloping stallion while using both hands to hold his rifle on his shoulder. If she weren't so head over heels in love with Shawn, she might...her brain stumbled to a halt on that thought, and she had to force down the panic that threatened to come up from that admission.

Huddling back down, she winced at the bullet wound that must hurt like hell, a bullet he had taken for her. How could she help but fall in love? She'd been telling herself her life was back in Phoenix, the only place she'd ever known before coming to Mountain Bend. But did she really want to return to the rat race of the big city and her almost solitary life? There were young men a few feet away whom she'd never met, who didn't know her, yet they stood ready to defend her against a madman. Other than an aging priest, there was no one back home who would make such a sacrifice on her behalf.

Another shot rang out from the trees, followed by a deafening barrage of return fire from all six men that seemed to go on forever. Lisa huddled lower, shivering when a sudden, eerie silence fell, the acrid smell of gunpowder wafting through Shawn's open door.

"Is it over?"

Someone whistled, and Shawn nodded, rising from his crouched position. "It's over."

Dakota reached Shawn before Lisa could get out, wailing sirens and a cloud of dust heralding the arrival of more law enforcement and an ambulance. As much as she wanted to rush to his side, she stood back and let the paramedics see to his injury, not surprised when they insisted he needed to ride with them to the hospital to get stitched up.

Two sheriff's officers, one young and lean, the other older with a middle-aged waistline, approached with grim faces.

"Is he dead, then?" Shawn asked, holding his hand out to Lisa.

The older man nodded. "They don't come deader." He tipped his hat to Lisa. "Ma'am, as soon as you're up to it, I'll need you to come in and make a statement. Are you up to looking at him and giving us an ID?"

"I'll try, but I doubt if I know him," she said, looking at the stretcher two men carried from the woods, the body covered with a blanket.

"Let's get this done then you can ride with me to the hospital."

If for no other reason than to move Shawn along in getting the medical help he needed, she didn't hesitate to step forward as the sheriff lowered the blanket from the man's face. "No, I'm sorry. I've never seen him before."

"That's okay. We had to check. You two get going. We'll search him and the car and get his name soon enough."

"Thanks, Lyle."

"You can thank me by healing fast and getting on the campaign trail."

"Campaign trail?" Lisa asked, climbing into the back of the ambulance behind Shawn then giving Dakota a grateful smile as he strode up. "I really appreciate..."

He cut her off with a hand slice. "No need. We take care of our own." Turning his black eyes on Shawn, he said, "Clayton and I will meet you there," before walking back to his horse.

Lisa kept quiet as she sat next to Shawn, and he closed his eyes, leaning his head against the padded side of the van as it started rolling. All too aware he'd never mentioned their relationship was anything except a temporary affair, she hugged her newfound feelings to herself and made plans on where to go from here.

****

Shawn stomped up to the front door of Lisa's duplex, trying his best not to lay into her for slipping away from the clinic last night when he'd been groggy with pain meds. After refusing to let the ambulance take him all the way into Boise, they'd agreed to drop him at the small medical clinic in Mountain Bend that stayed open late for emergencies. Just as he'd suspected, the bullet had gone through the fleshy part of his upper arm, requiring minor cleaning up and a few sutures. That hadn't kept Drew and Jen from joining Clayton and Dakota, or the entire sheriff's department from converging on the clinic. That Lisa had taken advantage of the chaos to leave unnoticed still rankled.

Upon discovering she'd returned here instead of his place, he'd waited to confront her and to bring her news until school let out today and he knew she'd be home. He wasn't sure how she'd take to what Lyle and Clayton had learned about her stalker, the personal connection sure to break her heart. The stalking alone had taken a huge toll on her, to hear it was a blood relative would bother anyone.

He rapped on the door then let himself in when he tried the knob.

"Shawn." Lisa rushed forward from the kitchen,

surprised pleasure turning her face rosy. "Shouldn't you be resting?"

"I'm fine, Lisa, as I told you yesterday." Tossing his hat onto the sofa, he stalked toward her with narrowed eyes, his lips curling as she backed up with a wary look until she bumped the counter. "You snuck out last night without a word." He caged her in by bracing his hands on the counter behind her.

"You needed your rest."

"Lame, Lisa, very lame. I needed you, and you weren't there." Leaning down, he brushed her lips before sliding his mouth down her neck. "To make matters worse, you weren't there when I got home. Why?"

"I wasn't sure..." She tilted her head, giving him easier access to her soft skin.

"About what?" he murmured, stroking her pulse with his tongue.

"I can't think straight when you do that."

He nipped the tender spot between shoulder and neck, liking the easy access the scooped neckline of her blouse offered. If he didn't have more pressing matters to discuss with her, he'd forgo talk altogether. "Try."

"Well, you never said anything about me staying after....afterward. How was I supposed to know where you wanted me?"

"You know, Lisa," he said, lifting his head to give her a close, direct stare, "you're quite a contradictory person. There are times you have no problem speaking your mind, and others when you shy away from asking a simple question."

Frowning, she placed her hands on his chest but

didn't attempt to push him away. Maybe she was learning how immovable he could be about certain things. Hoping to catch her off guard, he stated, "We'll work on that, but I'm warning you, it might take months, years even for me to straighten you out."

"Huh?" Her eyes rounded in a dumbfounded expression. "What are you saying?"

"I'm saying if you love me half as much as I love you, we're looking at a lifetime of working on your issues. *Ah shit.*" Pulling her into his arms, he stroked her long, blonde hair. "No tears. My heart's been through enough in the last thirty-six hours."

"I think," she hiccupped, "I love you a lot more than half."

"Excellent. Come sit with me. I have news." He ushered her over to the sofa and settled her on his lap.

"You know who he was," she stated stiffly.

"Yes, and it won't be easy to hear. His name was Bruce Pomeroy, and he was your half-brother, and, until recently, the only heir to a fortune."

She drew back, her brows dipped in a perplexed look. "I don't have...my father's son?"

"Yes, almost two decades older than you, and his father, whom Lyle has talked to, is Frank Pomeroy." He went on to relate what the senior Pomeroy had told Lyle, not surprised when she adamantly shook her head when he mentioned her inheritance.

"No, no way. I want nothing from him. That ship sailed when my mother died young, working herself to the bone to provide for us. I won't let him use me to assuage his late-in-life guilt for abandoning his responsibility to her and me."

"Okay." He understood her attitude and wouldn't push her. She needed time to digest everything. It just happened he had the perfect way to distract her from thinking too hard on the fact her own brother had wanted her dead.

"Your shoulder!" Lisa exclaimed as he surged to his feet with her in his arms and headed for the bedroom.

"Is fine, but you can kiss it, for starters, if it'll make you feel better."

She kicked off her shoes as they reached the hall, whispering in his ear, "Yes, Sir, it definitely will."

EPILOGUE

Phoenix, two months later

Lisa paused on the threshold of the large, stately home and rubbed her sweaty palms down the sides of her white cotton slacks. She'd debated for an hour over what to wear, but since this was her first experience with meeting a parent who had been absent from her entire life, she'd opted for cool and casual. She rang the bell then turned, taking one more look at Shawn and Father Joe who stood leaning against Shawn's packed SUV.

Her heart turned over, the sight of the two most important people in her life giving her that boost of courage she needed to see this through. Father hadn't stopped beaming since they popped in on him as soon as she and Shawn had arrived in Phoenix last week. To say he was pleased with seeing them together and hearing they were staying together was an understatement. Telling herself the priest was the only parent she needed at this stage of her life helped her make the decision to give in to Frank Pomeroy's pleas for them to meet. Of course, Father's lecture on "to err is human, to forgive, divine" also chipped away at her reasons for having nothing to do with the man.

But it was knowing she would be returning to Idaho with Shawn, living with him on his ranch, and starting a full-time job teaching second grade in the fall that bolstered her into agreeing to come here today. They'd cleared out her apartment, getting rid of anything that didn't fit in the cruiser, and she'd enjoyed lunch with her former principal to turn in her resignation. All that was left was to ease an old man's conscience.

One side of the tall double doors opened, and Shawn gave her a thumbs-up as she pivoted and entered the cool foyer.

"Hello, Ms. Halldor," the smiling, plump woman wearing a maid's uniform greeted her. "Mr. Pomeroy is waiting for you in the sitting room, if you'll follow me."

The white marble floor gleamed, and Lisa wondered how it was kept so clean and shiny when she entered a white carpeted room and saw Frank Pomeroy seated in a wheelchair by the marble fireplace. Before she had time to question why anyone would need a fireplace in Phoenix, he beckoned her forward with a wave of one gnarled hand.

"Come in, come in. Let me look at you. Regina, bring us some refreshments."

"Please, don't go to any trouble. I can't stay long. There are people waiting for me." Sucking in a breath, she crouched in front of the wheelchair, grateful she resembled her mother. "I just stopped by to tell you I'm sorry about your son, and to reiterate I don't want anything from you. I hope you'll honor my wishes."

An investigation into Bruce Pomeroy's finances revealed his massive debt from gambling and living beyond his already considerable means. She couldn't imagine Frank's pain,

knowing his only son had cherished money more

than human life.

"You have your mother's eyes." His hand trembled as he fingered the ends of her blonde hair. "And her hair color, so light."

Cocking her head, she asked, "You remember her, my mother?"

"Vaguely, more now that I've seen you. There were a lot of women in those days," he answered with blunt honesty. "I was a different man back then, and I'm paying the price for my selfish ways now. Growing old alone is..." He swallowed and blinked watery eyes. "Hard, very hard."

Broken. That was the word that came to Lisa's mind as she looked at the once-selfish man who had sired her. She didn't hate him, couldn't if she tried, and for the first time since hearing about him, she let herself feel compassion for him .

"I can't change that for you, but, for starters, why don't you get involved with worthwhile projects, charities that could use your contributions?"

His shoulders slumped. "You're so generous, where my son, my son...how did I go so wrong with him?"

Lisa stood, laying a hand on his shoulder. "I plan to return to Phoenix every few months. If you want, I'll make time to come by and stay longer."

Gratitude suffused his lined face. "I would like that. At least now I know I accomplished one decent thing in my life...I had you."

Lisa found her own way out and stepped into the bright Arizona sunshine with a lighter heart. Walking toward her future, she thought it had never looked more promising.

The End

ABOUT BJ WANE

I live in the Midwest with my husband and our Goldendoodle. I love dogs, enjoy spending time with my daughter, grandchildren, reading and working puzzles.

We have traveled extensively throughout the states, Canada and just once overseas, but I now much prefer being homebody.

I worked for a while writing articles for a local magazine but soon found my interest in writing for myself peaking.

My first book was strictly spanking erotica, but I slowly evolved to writing steamy romance with a touch of suspense. My favorite genre to read is suspense.

I love hearing from readers. Feel free to contact me at bjwane@cox.net with questions or comments.

MORE BOOKS BY BJ WANE

VIRGINIA BLUEBLOODS SERIES
Blindsided
Bind Me to You
Surrender to Me
Blackmailed
Bound by Two

MURDER ON MAGNOLIA ISLAND
Logan
Hunter
Ryder

MIAMI MASTERS SERIES
Bound and Saved
Master Me, Please
Mastering Her Fear
Bound to Submit
His to Master and Own
Theirs To Master

COWBOY DOMS SERIES
Submitting to the Rancher
Submitting to the Sheriff
Submitting to the Cowboy
Submitting to the Lawyer
Submitting to Two Doms
Submitting to the Cattleman
Submitting to the Doctor

COWBOY WOLF SERIES
Gavin
Cody
Drake

SINGLE TITLES
Claiming Mia
Masters of the Castle: Witness Protection Program
Dangerous Interference
Returning to Her Master
Her Master at Last

CONTACT BJ WANE

Website
bjwaneauthor.com

Twitter
twitter.com/bj_wane

Facebook
www.facebook.com/bj.wane
www.facebook.com/BJWaneAuthor

Bookbub
www.bookbub.com/profile/bj-wane

Instagram
www.instagram.com/bjwaneauthor

Goodreads
www.bit.ly/2S6Yg9F

Printed in Great Britain
by Amazon

40462397R00123